Hemorrhaging Slave of an Obese Eunuch

T0315991

Tom Bradley

First edition published by

Dog Horn Publishing
editor@doghornpublishing.com
doghornpublishing.com

CONTENTS:

Fricasseed Filipina

Elementary spirits are like children: they torment chiefly those who trouble about them... it is these who frequently occasion our bizarre or disturbing dreams... but they can manifest no thought other than our own... They reproduce good and evil indifferently, for they are without free will and are hence irresponsible; they exhibit themselves to ecstatics and somnambulists under incomplete and fugitive forms... Such creatures are neither damned nor guilty; they are curious and innocent. We may use or abuse them like animals or children.
—Eliphas Levi, *Dogme et Rituel de la Haute Magie*

It's a glorious Easter Sunday morning in Hiroshima Cathedral's parking lot. Sam Edwine is wedged behind the wheel of a bashed-up Mazda sub-compact, just trying to accomplish a little sleep.

Meanwhile, almost directly underneath the car's crumbling differential, deep in the demon-rife blackness of the cathedral crypt, Sam's wife squats with a coven of expatriate papists, taking certain purgatory-avoidance measures better left unimagined.

It's a bad surprise when one of Sam's bloodshot eyes pops open of its own accord just in time to witness a manifestation. Some wisps of Boom Town's brownish nitrogen dioxides swirl together with a bushel of airborne diesel particles and coalesce into a tiny center of consciousness.

Wandering tentatively around the churchyard, it approaches the Mazda and rattles a burnt-crisp knuckle against the windshield.

"Oh, I'm sorry, Dr. Edwine. Did I awaken you?"

Sam is too horrified to respond.

"Please forgive my appearance. I'm just trying to do my Paschal duty. It's the first time since I botched the flame dance that I've had the courage to come here."

When Sam reaches out a trembling hand to verify the existence of this salamander, it shrinks away, hissing, *"Noli me tangere,"* and disappears into dark billows of carbonized hemp fiber. Floating and chattering, it envelops the Mazda, smudging the windows.

"I can't shake your hand, professor," comes the muffled whisper from between wads and folds of this strange fabric. The stuff has been configured vaguely to resemble the indigenous garb of a nearby island-nation which, through the expedient of sex slavery, provides oceans of orgasms for the grandsons of Great God Hirohito.

"My body is unlucky now," says the wraith, peeking out and flashing a toothless rictus. "The Yakuza pimps won't touch someone tainted with death, and they aren't fond of freelancers. So they refuse to sponsor the renewal of my entertainer's visa."

These words slough off in threads, and slip beneath the car, to emanate from the beer cans under the seat. Now they unwind from among the stash of methedrine-dusted joints in the glove compartment. And now they radiate in a web from Sam's own lumbar ganglia.

"I am an outright illegal alien. Immigration is after me, and just because of my vocation I'm unloved by the municipal authorities. So I must disguise myself as what I truly am by birth. Nobody would ever suspect me of voluntarily joining such an oppressed minority."

The exotic garment looks more like a transient's rags than a formerly indentured sex slave's work clothes. But the butter-fingered flame dancer seems to feel an emotional attachment to it, so Sam says nothing.

"All by myself, I've introduced a new kink to the local salary-men. They pretend to re-rape my people, in emulation of their proud forbears. My third-degree burns make it all the more titillating for them to pay homage to the spirits of their revered ancestors."

The baked child rematerializes for a moment in order to glance down at herself. "I know it's not in the best of taste," she says, smoothing away a few wrinkles and dust particles. "But it's the only halfway decent outfit I have."

"I think you look nice," says Sam, wondering why she lingers. It's almost chow-time around the subterranean altar. Meat's on.

She inspects her invisible reflection in Sam's side-view mirror, adjusts her costume, and ruffles up the few filaments of black floss that have managed to sprout from the mass of broiled tissue that once was her scalp. She lifts her ashen blouse and presents a scabby, scrawny, ribby torso.

"I may have stayed away from here a long time, but I can kneel a lot longer than any of those pious people—and on cobblestones too."

Then, bravely, like a small phoenixed Maid of Orleans, she limps toward the concrete steps that plunge into the crypt chapel.

Suddenly, grunts and howls filter up through the pavement in lascivious descant, as from Milton's asphaltic Hell. Eucharistic racket, Mrs. Edwine shrieking on top, freezes the flame dancer in her tracks, and she begins to weep.

"I want to pray!" she wails.

Sam unfolds himself from the Mazda and stands by her side, not two feet from the steps—closer than this husky atheist has ever gotten. He mutters, "You're only a few steps away from sanctuary. Enter now into the One, Holy, Catholic, Apostolic, Romish, and jab like that."

Sam himself, of course, will never go down there, not as long as he remains uncremated. At his mother's knee, little Sammy learned the definition of the word *simile* by coolly considering the nicety of the wine and bread. On the other hand, each Sabbath his otherwise rational wife trembles before a wafer-thin slice of the sole material that puts her in divergence with post seventeenth-century thought. It would be not only disrespectful, but insane to approach something that substantial with a head full of attitudes flip as Sam's.

"Don't worry," he repeats, cringing from the brink. "You look real nice."

"But I'm ashamed." She holds up melted, webbed, nail-less hands and tries to cover a noseless face. "There was no time for rehearsal because the salary-men were getting impatient. I did my best, Dr. Edwine, but my arms weren't strong enough for the benzine goblets!"

"Never mind," says Sam. "We all have our spastic moments. My own asshole is fluttering pretty bad right now. Besides, these mackerel-snappers are obligated to accept you. You won't be the first Magdalen they've embraced. See? Father Itchy-Nookie or whatever is down there, all suited up in his prettiest rhinestone dress and big glans penis hat, and he beckons you to come on down. Don't keep him waiting."

Sam turns on his heel—or tries to. He must say his goodbyes. Subtly, he will fuck off back into the car and roll up the windows tightly, before his wife's father confessor sprouts goat horns and granny teats and breaks out the meat cleaver.

"You never come to Mass," comes the voice, lisping. The little whore's waxing all shy and babyish now, plying professional skills other than terpsichorean. "If you come, too, everybody will be so surprised they won't notice me."

Try as he might, Sam can't seem to disentangle their elbows. But the paralysis doesn't extend all the way up to his tongue and teeth and lips; so, teetering vertiginously over his would-be seductress, he tries to start a conversation that will last through the benediction and the recessional and obviate this whole horrible fucking moment of truth in a stampede of shriven faithful. He commences babbling through a parched mouth—

"See the finger bowl thing down there with the heavily rouged plaster-of-Paris Barbie doll perched on it? That's full of valid-but-illicit holy water that exists but isn't supposed to be wet,

8

except it is anyway, and you moisten your pulse points ever so slightly with—"

"That's not holy water, Dr. Edwine. It's baptismal water, and you're not allowed to put your fingers in the font."

"So, you're a blood-guzzler, too, eh? You know, my mom baptized me a low-church Epis—"

Gray tears of plasmatic lymph begin to flop from under a pair of out-of-mesh eyelids.

"Oh, come on," moans Sam. "Don't make me feel like an ogre. If you're hell-bent on making communion, little Missy, you'll have to shuffle up that aisle under your own steam. My whole, hefty metabolism recoils like an albino vampire from the Real Presence. Why do you reckon I spend my Sundays snoozing up here in the parking lot?"

Nevertheless, the creature pulls him toward the pit. He wrenches his hand away and turns to flee. But the flame dancer's arm suddenly grows sumo muscles, and the good doctor is beneath the surface of this planet before his knees can lock.

* * * *

The blackened Filipina flits on scorched crow wings, shedding benzine goblets left and right, which explode like tactical thermonuclear devices.

Father Itchy-Nookie lurks simultaneously in all the crannies of this catacomb, his clutch purse brimming with transubstantial gore—Sam knows this without separating either seizured set of eyelids. To the assembled expatriate congregation, Hiroshima's chief attorney of nothingness dispenses wads of gristle and scab, flopping them greasily from the chipped rim of a crude ceramic chalice. And, unlike Sam's present interlocutor, the wads are not even properly cooked.

Like a Baphometic cocktail party, the Catholics, Mrs. Edwine included, squat in vulgar positions around the altar, play with themselves, and trepan their own children with ragged thumbnails.

9

Sam rises from their midst, not looking quite like himself. It's almost as though a fraternal twin is standing in for him, disguised in his occidental-style beard and rumpled academic clothes. Not forgetting to genuflect piously, he climbs behind the altar, upsetting the cross.

His spouse and the other Mariolators choose the moment of the professor's leavetaking to yowl, in un-American Popish Esperanto, a cannibal hymn in the mixolydian mode—

> *Pluck forth thy royal diadems,*
> *pluck forth thy locks entwined within,*
> *pluck forth from radiant brows the flesh*
> *which pads the seams where headbones mesh.*

Sam crawls into a hidden recess in the wall and rummages among a gaudy treasure-trove of sacred objects and other such assorted jiggery-popery: pyxes, monstrances, reliquaries, crucifixes, icons, ruby-studded rosaries.

> *Pry back thy scalp like fecund sod,*
> *expose thy rank farm's protein pods,*
> *chip free thy skull, let marrow drain*
> *till one grey tegument remains.*

Mrs. Edwine's warbling soprano and the snarls of the elementary spirits gradually blend together with Sam's seismic snores, and transmogrify themselves into the whining of a tiny internal combustion engine at full throttle.

> *And when thy brain is amply shown,*
> *and naught is left of skin and bone,*
> *then serve thyself to Christus Rex,*
> *or suffer our collective hex.*

After an indefinite period of time Sam emerges, looking different again. On the anterior portion of his skull he displays the face of Grünewald's Saint Anthony, cheeks, forehead and scalp stretched like rubber by talons and beaks. Shouldering a golden shovel, he heads for the exit, a flashlight of purest platinum poking from his pocket. But, before vanishing, he turns and addresses the ravening parishioners in a voice other than his own.

"I have memories stored up, good and bad. But mostly neutral."

Hemorrhaging Slave of an Obese Eunuch

From the tambourine I have eaten.
From the cymbal I have drunk.
I have borne the cup of gonads.
The room I have entered.
—Firmicus Maternus

I thought muscle mass was supposed to decline with the emptying of the scrotum. But here I found a pair of muscles thriving on the vast sides of my castrated traveling companion. I was surprised, yet had no complaints. They provided life-saving handholds for me, these living flexures of human steak.

Like most lifelong residents of the capital city, I'm not fond of salt water, especially in large amounts. I react like a blind Greekling cat to the sea, even a sea calm and balmy as the one in which we shipwrecked. When the brine received our little party, I grabbed my traveling companion in panic. Call it an emergency suspension of the hands-off policy which normally governs my relationship with Spado. That's the obese eunuch's peculiar name—and, no, we are not lovers, he and I. (Gender-specific pronouns will be employed advisedly in this account.)

I'm being too dramatic when I say *shipwrecked*. It was no wreck, properly speaking, not even a ship. Our becalmed boat just came spontaneously apart at the seams or joints or whatever they're called, for reasons a landlubber like me will never know.

When our craft dissolved, I decided I was already dead, and reached for Spado by reflex. Sort of a valedictory grope. I expected my hands to find no firmer purchase than a drunken reveler can expect when he stands up too quickly at a banquet, falls head-first into the middle of the table, and tries to break his fall on the sebaceous flanks of the roasted sow. But here, under the rolls and rolls of gelding pudge, I found my special pair of salvation-grips.

These two muscles were hard as I imagine a certain skull to have been. The dome of bone belonged to an Illyrian witch who'd supplied Spado with the hairdo that came unplaited from pretty purple ribbons as our boat melted. Her reddish-blond tresses tumbled about his whale-sized shoulders and dangled damply down in my eyes.

I'm exaggerating for effect. Spado's rib-woven muscles aren't really quite as hard as a barbarian hag's peeled cranium. But anything firm feels adamantine to a man who can't swim, who finds himself up to the nostrils in liquid, no solidity in sight.

Nautical nemesis overtook us at a leisurely pace. Spado, me attached, was able gradually to ease into the watery part of the world, one temperature-testing toe at a time. He was soothed, like a baby in bath water; he gurgled and chuckled. No sea holds terrors for a suckling whale. To me it felt sickly warmish, as one imagines amniotic fluid to be, or maybe recollects it to have been. That notion deepened my revulsion. I never want to get sucked back again into the filthy syrup of the womb. I've had more than sufficient existence this time around.

The sky was vacant and paralyzed, an intimation of rigor mortis. There was nothing by way of meteorology to hasten our boat's demise. Nevertheless, it disintegrated efficiently as Nero's mother's did a few years ago, on that Feast of Minerva which was almost her last, but not quite, no thanks to her boat-sabotaging matricide of a son. The thought of that glamorous dame dunked in a nearly identical predicament inspired my traveling companion. He began to perform the broad sort of theatrics favored by the neutered classes in all times and places.

"I am Agrippina," he moaned in a matronly contralto, "mother of the Imperial, um, *Dictator*. And that pot-bellied, red-headed bastard son of mine has fucked me again. This time figuratively." Observing my panicked behavior from beneath disdainful eyelids, he added, "Cleave to Agrippina's sacrosanct bo-

13

bosom if you must. But do it with dignity and discretion, as befits a natural-born citizen of Rome."

I can explain Spado's seaworthiness no better than I can our boat's lack of that quality, unless it has something to do with the near total fluidity of the castrato himself. Apart from my handholds, he was already a drink of water. I've seen Lebanese lads playing in the gentle eastern swell, who are able to recline at ease on the surface like olive oil freighters with amphorae overturned among the ballast. But Spado's buoyancy was of another order. The sea didn't hold him at arm's length, but received him like a part of itself, and held him in suspension. His body held such a high ratio of fluid to meat that he only needed to relax all four limbs to bob vertically like a soggy cork, meanwhile keeping me from sinking to death. No treading water for this testicle-unencumbered traveling companion of mine.

His lower limbs, which were nearly as long as the entirety of me, were dropsied to a degree only manageable on such extended shinbones. This, like excessive vertical growth itself, could be a mysterious side effect of unsexing. I'll have to check Elder Pliny if I ever get within reach of a library again. Perhaps fluid retention is a result of the sumptuous diet adopted by the minority of eunuchs who maintain the vitality to overindulge in anything beyond whining. Or do their bodies reabsorb unreleased seminal fluid and turn it to blubber in compensation for sexual deprivation? But who in my acquaintance is less deprived in that department than lascivious Spado? He's a walking, writhing demythologization of the female orgasm. I kept that in mind while riding the sea wrapped around this member of the so-called third sex. I suspect a fourth, and possibly a fifth, should be added, to accommodate Spado.

"Ah, me!" cried our Empress Mother. "I fear my coiffure might not survive such a drastic rinse!" He shook placental broth from his halo of hair, which remained brightly sunset-colored as the evening that Illyrian witch's scalp had been teased off, expertly stretched and tanned. Entwined among the purloined curls was a

14

sardine skeleton. I'm not sure if my traveling companion had placed it there deliberately, or if it was a love-present from some admiring porpoise. But it did create a certain enhancement, like an exquisite barrette carved of the finest Gangetic ivory.

I apologize. In spite of that extravagant simile, which slipped out from I don't know where, please rest assured that your narrator is no sensual person. Call me anachronistic, but I have always done my best to hew to the stoical line of our Republican grandfathers. (Rather, *my* Republican grandfathers—who knows whence the obese eunuch sprang?) For example, I will be unable to tell you if my frantically burrowing fingers tickled Spado. I lack experience in this sort of thing. On our wanderings till now we had, by tacit agreement, kept bodily contact at a minimum. It was frank trepidation on my part. Spado's motivation, assuming there was one, remained unclear. I hope it wasn't revulsion—I'm not the handsomest creature in the Empire.

It's not altogether impossible, I suppose, that he was aroused in some barely imaginable way by the newfound intimacy between himself and the tiny toad who clung to him like a twig in a Baetican flash flood. In any case, he chose the moment of our first touch to flex his pillar-thick spine, to gape up into the deathly lapis lazuli of the sky, to gulp down a few voluminous breaths, to ratchet up his female impersonation, and to commence shrieking.

"Oh! Oh!" he trilled, ever so cheerfully. "Adrift in uncharted waters! Anchorless! Rudderless! The planet's curvature affording no Calypso-enchanted Ogygia!"

"Excuse me?" I managed to burble and gag.

"Help La Agrippina! For I am she, and none other, and I founder! Won't someone rescue grand me and my loyal, um, *entourage*, so to speak? Where is that poopoo-bottomed slave of mine, anyway?"

"Graptus? Haven't seen him lately."

"Well, there's nothing for it but to forget him and save ourselves, like Nero's soggy momsy before us. We—rather, *I*—must swim for it, meanwhile consoling myself with the knowledge that we are privileged to suffer the same fate as that elegant society matron and her lady-in-waiting. You be What's-her-name."

"What's whose name?"

"My lady-in-waiting. You know, the one who took the vindictive hireling boatman's oar right in the forehead, rather than let it brain beloved me, her mistress. You be stout, loyal What's-her-whatever."

"Aceronia?"

"Is that what they called her?" yawned Spado, already indifferent. No need to sprain any emotive tendons. His performance, after all, was being appreciated by no audience in particular.

Passing vessels were scarce as beaches and cliffs in this zone of the Adriatic, if Adriatic it still was. The horizon was a perfect circle all around, flat and featureless as a burnished brass mirror, bile-green. Bile-scented as well. The only sounds other than the queenly ones coming from Spado's mouth were the seismic rumbles of king-sized viscera within his torso, against which my left ear was suction-cupped. Still, if I hadn't been inhaling kelp at the moment, I would have begged my friend to blaspheme Caesar's deified *mater* more quietly. Even here in the middle of nowhere, aping a member of the imperial family smacked too dangerously of *lese majestie* to suit me. As a citizen, I could be beheaded or throttled for such indiscretion, or quietly poisoned. Crucifixion, on the other hand, would be the prescribed legal procedure for Spado. Did the tree exist capable of yielding a transverse beam sturdy enough?

"Please, please, dear Heavens," the Empress Mother was crying, "won't some brawny sailor with pecs way out to here—no, make that *here*—come rowing randomly along? Won't he reach down and salvage this trusty old uterus of mine, from which sprang the current Autocrat of the Known World? More or less? I mean, not including Ethiopia and Parthia. Shit-holes."

"Don't forget India," I said. "And the Land of Silk."

"Yes, yes, good point. India and Silky Land are definitely not shit-holes."

"You can tell from their dry goods."

It may seem odd, but I can banter in the middle of a panic. My only strength and steadfastness, the only skill that kept me from succumbing to Nero's penchant for casual slaughter back home, is to be found on the tip of my tongue. My eyes can be swirling in their sockets, my heart can be thumping louder than a Thuringian swiving his milch cow, and my mouth can chit-chat. There'll be no indication of anything amiss besides a certain raising of the pitch of my admittedly reedy voice. It's one of the minor Roman virtues, I suppose, glibness under pressure.

No stranger to chit-chat himself, Spado was slipping into one of the talking fits which individuals of his physical type are prone to: "I wouldn't mind being crowned the drowning momsy of the Autocrat of India and Silky Land, but I'd submit to being the floating *turd* of the powerless puppet vassal of neither Ethiopia nor, especially, fucky-*icky* Parthia, and I really don't—"

Etcetera. High as a woman's, loud as a bull's, Spado's voice, like the rest of him, was three-fourths false, one quarter real. But I'm grateful to have grown intimate with one unfeigned thing about him—two things, actually. They were to be encountered midway between his depilated armpits and the cartwheel-sized nipples that pouted from his udders. The Greeklings in Alexandria have surely given these anatomical features an official name, but I'm not aware of it. I fastened my whole personality to that rippling pair of muscles, my pudge-submerged, skull-hard handholds.

Spado was not unresponsive. "As the parent of your sovereign," he murmured down into my ear, "I command you not to squirm and whimper quite so much. Passersby could get the wrong idea about us."

"What passersby? What *idea*? I'm just trying not to die immediately."

These particular muscles, like all the others, are imperceptible to palpitation on my own scrawny body. I have only seen them developed to any comparable degree in Nubians mustered out of detachments of mercenary spearmen and conscripted to bear the

17

palanquins of eastern client kings, come to the capital city in embassies. If, under the layers of fluid fat, the rest of our obese eunuch's physique is developed like this, it explains how, with a single back-handed, absent-minded swipe, he could knock his luckless slave out cold in a hail of splintered teeth.

Speaking of Graptus, Spado slipped out of character just long enough to inquire once again as to his manservant's whereabouts: "Where is that feeble-minded spaniel fucker?"

"I lost sight of him at about the same time as the last bit of land."

"Then I shall have to throw myself entirely into your custodial care, my loyal, stout lady-in—what's it again?"

"Aceronia." I tried not to sigh.

"Yes, that's it. You are *such* a dear! So gladly did you die rather than allow the mussing of my electrum-radiant curls!" Spado raised his fingers, which seemed long and thick as my forearms, and ran them through the Illyrian witch's hair, combing out several of the lower forms of sea life. "You know, don't you, loving Aceronia, that the Sun God envied this, my crowning glory? You can see why. It puts him to shame at midsummer's highest noon. So he sent my demon asshole incestuous prick of a son to try to darken my 'do with blood and brain matter. But you foiled the plan by offering up your own mousy thatch! Snuggly Aceronia! Don't think I'll forget when we stand together and testify before Rhadamanthy-whoozit, Judge of the Dead. Which should be any moment now, and—*oooh!* I'm frightening you, aren't I? Better not squeeze much harder than that, dear. You might puncture me. Your Empress-Momsy's just a tissue of skin, after all, like anyone else. But, if I do say so myself, mine is the most unsinkable tissue of skin west of Zeugma on the Euphrates, where the ferrymen inflate goat bladders and affix them for flotation to the sides of their reed rafts, and—"

And so on. Roles could be assigned and played at leisure, as no particular attention needed to be paid to the preservation of our lives. Spado had only to scull a thigh occasionally, or perhaps

18

to affect a languid thwartwise paddle of a thigh-thick forearm once in a very long while, to propel us. The direction he propelled us was a single one, but otherwise a matter of indifference. I almost began to allow myself to entertain the possibility that watery death was not guaranteed today.

Just as my hands relaxed a bit, the obese eunuch began voluptuously to weep. Right on schedule. One learns to expect radical mood shifts in eunuchs. A wet nurse could time milkings by them.

"Ah, the lady Agrippina! Was there ever such a goddess? Even in death she was capable of inspiring erotic poetry from her ungrateful brat." Spado's eyes unloaded a few barrels of salt water down onto my head, as if there weren't plenty of that around already. "Wail for me, fish-reeky Aphrodite of the waves! I am getting puckery about the gills! The Divine Queen Dowager is taking on water! Blub-blub!"

He went under for dramatic effect, dragging me down with him. My reaction must have persuaded him that particular piece of stage business wasn't worth the bother. I fear my fingernails might've raked some stripes from the lushness of the imperial epidermis.

Everyone will have noticed a definite histrionic bent in these gelding priests, or priestesses, or what-have-you, of the Ineffable Goddess. (That is Spado's divine vocation, in case you've been wondering.) At a tender age they are given a sharp shard of Anatolian pottery and somehow persuaded that it would be a good idea to deprive themselves of the proper outlet for theatrical impulses: namely, the testes. This unmanning renders them prone to affectation. They spend the rest of their lives slipping into impromptu impersonations of distinguished historical personages, invariably female, *e.g.*, horse-fornicating Semiramis, family-butchering Medea, our own nymphomaniacal Messalina.

You can hear these smooth-crotched functionaries swishing down a crowded street several blocks away. It's as if they don't care to distinguish themselves from the debased pantomime "artists" who defile the public stage with false bosoms, falsetto squawks and real flatulence. In their social climbing mode, on the other hand, this priesthood tones it down a bit, and tries to affect effete aesthetism. They aspire to the condition of the wealthy pathics who, swathed in transparent silk gauze, have draped themselves and their loose anuses around the Palatine colonnades since the accession of Agrippina's hideous son.

"Spado—I mean, Agrippina?"

"What?"

"You can't be divine if you haven't died yet."

"Poetic license. You be quiet down there."

"Recall that your son could only have you legally deified after he succeeded in murdering you. And you turned out to be such a good swimmer that he finally had to encompass it via thugs with clubs, while you were in bed, high but not necessarily dry."

"Yet here I am, undrowned, unclubbed, unbedded (unfortunately), *and* divine, all at once. And you are my lady-in-waiting, the movingly loyal What's-her-cunting-face. You will speak only when spoken to. Besides, you have an oar sunken into your forehead, and your brains are forming a discolored slick all around us. It's so off-putting. Where's Graptus booger-nose? How dare he leave me unattended?"

"Your valet has vanished."

"Popped under the throbbing horizon," murmured Spado, getting morose so abruptly he almost threw me off like a balking donkey. He scanned the sea pensively and mused on his bereavement. "Can I recall a time when dearly departed Graptus wasn't wiping my ass for me?" He sighed, sucked on his full lips, and spigoted on the tears again, albeit in a dutiful, slightly bored way.

Then the melancholy trance passed, and he got all gruff and deep-voiced (as much as possible, in his under-equipped condition). With the rough affection of a mannish type, a stoic spirit too full of old-timey Republican *virtu* to give way to something as effeminate as grief, Spado bass-baritone belched, "Damn Graptus' eyes, har-*rummph*. Good lad, though, all in all. Stout. Butch. A better man than—well. Let's not go too far. Now we'll have to grope our

20

way to who-knows-where without a pack animal to abuse for fun. Not that we have much to pack anymore. It's all on the sea bottom. Except for my, er, handsome, rugged, manly toupee here." A grin spread across Spado's mile-wide face. "Not to mention a certain item far too precious to have been strapped baggage-wise on any retarded slave's bony shoulders. If you know what I mean."

He nudged me under the water and winked broadly, with a loud squishy sound from between satchel-sized eyelids. I knew exactly what he meant, and the item was indeed precious. It was also gone. My heart sank to depths lower even than those which plummeted under our feet. I couldn't speak for guilt. That item—that *jar*, to be specific—was my sole responsibility, not Graptus', and I'd let a measly shipwreck distract me to the point of losing it. Spado's sanguine view of the universe allowed him to assume I still had the jar secreted about my person. That was a silly assumption, because every bit of my person was secreted about his, and he would have felt the hard ceramic lump against his belly.

Concentration not being a strong point among those with emptied scrota (another mysterious side effect), he snapped out of his butch mode and giggled, "Mind if I go wee-wee? No? Yes? Ask me if I care." Then he tried to engage me in some speculative historiography. "Aceronia! What an ambiguous way to make your mark in history! Did you cry out to bring upon yourself the skull-splitting oar, or the succoring arms, of the sailor whom Nero hired to finish us off? Did you hanker after soft or rough treat-ment?"

"Don't tell me. You're about to say something like, 'Maybe Aceronia was game for both.'"

"Yes, and was just taking the luck of the draw."

"And she paid the price."

"Or got the reward."

"An oar through the forehead is a reward?"

"You never know," leered Spado. "That final breath could be a brain-suffocating orgasm, the kind that makes even the Inef-fable Goddess get moist and grunt. An assassin's oar may feel nic-

nicer, deep inside your noggin, than a scrumptious food tidbit feels inside your tummy. For example, a perfect mushroom with red cap. And white spots. Swimming in honey. If you take my *me-e-e-e-aning.*"

He nudged and winked again, and I did take his meaning. My heart, already fallen to the sea-bottom, began to burrow into the sediment, to hide for shame among the fish turds. Can you guess what spore-bearing food tidbits, preserved in honey, the lost jar contained?

Spado giggled, "Nero's boatman is navigating through someone's little head. Feel his toadstool paddle? That wet wood, those salty knots, those cool, spongy splinters sloughing onto the interior walls of your cranium? They are your reward, Aceronia."

"You're drifting into climes where I can't follow."

"Yes, we salvation cultists are trained in fearless eschatological speculation. Speaking of which, you did salvage our precious honey-mushrooms, didn't you?"

Luckily for me, the grand dame didn't feel the need to wait for an answer.

"Let's have one each. For La Agrippina, in practical terms, that translates to a half-dozen sweet lovelies. You get exactly one. Or maybe a half, if you're willing to live up to that stoical ideal you're always prattling about. We need fortification for the journey to the realm of the dead shitty people. Probably my servant will be down there before us, just lazing mindlessly around, weak chin hanging slack, and I can re-kill him with a chop across the back of the neck, like *this!*"

For my edification Spado demonstrated the single downward swipe of his enormous left hand with which he intended to break Graptus' already dead neck. This stirred up the first tidal wave of our doldrummed voyage and nearly rinsed me off like a grain of sand from a navel. I'm sure I screamed and scratched.

It wasn't for loss of life that I screamed, but loss of fungus. Those mushrooms were my love. Preserved in the medium-grade produce of Mount Hymettus bees, they made the heavens turn inside out and switch places with the underworld and do backward somersaults behind my eyeballs. They made even an unassuming man like me loosen his traveling tunic and bellow, right along with the Spados of this world, "Fuck everything that doesn't conduce to guffawing—which is very little under the sun! And behind it, too!"

We'd gotten the delicacies an eternity ago, way back when the soles of our feet still knew the blessed sensation of Terra Mater—or at least the dreck that gets wedged under your sandal straps in Illyria (don't ask what we were doing there). Our supplier was the abovementioned witch, whose scalp full of Nero-colored curls was destined to be the single item we managed to salvage from our calamitous sea disaster a bit earlier today.

I don't like to talk about that screeching crone, and won't here, except to emphasize what I'm sure you already know: the more manual details of our dealings with her were left to Graptus. Call us social climbers if you like, but Spado and I both try to live up to the philosophical tradition that a gentleman never touches tools. So, the procurement and preparation of the master's wig were effected by the servile member of our "touring troupe," which is what Spado likes to call us. Frankly, we are more like a band of fugitives now, at least to the limited extent a fugitive condition is achievable in this increasingly anarchic quadrant of the Empire. An indifferent administrator, Agrippina's son is letting brigandage and piracy resurge. It's disgraceful.

"We could use a couple pirates around here," said Spado. "Hung pirates. And I'm not talking crosses, nails and diapers. Well, maybe diapers." Getting no response from me, he compressed his numerous chins upon his ox-yoke collarbones and aimed his face straight down. For the first time, he looked into my eyes and spoke neither freakishly high nor unnaturally low, but in his own tenor.

"I hope you're not troubling yourself to scrutinize the seascape for some sign of Graptus."

"He could still catch up," I offered.

"Sea monsters have already defleshed him, like this sardine that accentuates my bouffant so effectively."

"Many of the unfree are systematically dilatory. It's one of the ways they try to postpone our working them to death."

"I never managed to work Graptus a full day in his life. Nevertheless, he's dead, no doubt about it. My property came at a bargain, and I got what I paid for, and that is the way of the universe. Ask any religious authority. I guarantee that cut-rate-quality Graptus melted with the boat, for he was even more water-soluble than you. We're probably swimming in little discount chunks of him right now. Gross thought. Tighten one's cheeks."

Spado's point was gross, yes, but well taken. The slave's muscles were childlike, his stores of fat nonexistent, the skin that sagged over his brittle bones puckered and grandpa-gray. Elder Pliny has described that peculiar combination of pathologies. It's characteristic of wretches reared on the jejune diet of scrounged acorns in pre-agricultural regions, such as the backwater from whose animalistic bourne Graptus was snatched as a rooting runt.

"He may have been half-acorn," said Spado, "but he was no precious mushroom. So let's not dip him in honey. Let this be Graptus' threnody: mentally deficient, stunted, weak, inferior, he was, in a word, *Illyrian*."

Spado's pack animal coincidentally belonged to the same species as Spado's pelt animal. The drizzly dreariness of Illyria incubates such a languishing population, it's not unlikely the formerly red-headed witch was Graptus' own tribeswoman. She might have even been the one who sold him into bondage, time gone by.

I suppose all this sounds familiar to you: scrawny, no muscles to speak of, reedy voice, not the handsomest creature in the Empire. No, I'm not related to Graptus or his great auntie the bald conjuress. Spado's slave may have a twin somewhere in the Adriatic vicinity, but it's not your narrator. I'm Italian, from the proper side of this defining sea. And I've never eaten an acorn in my life, except in polenta mush. That's considered civilized cuisine if there's been a substandard wheat harvest. Perfectly permissible. I

24

have no intention of serving as a Graptus replacement—assuming he even needs one.

Nor am I an expert on Illyrian livestock. You'd have to ask Spado for further details of the, shall we say, *business* transacted between the pertinent pair of natives. In my capacity as potential poison-taster, I was the first member of our party to sample the mushrooms, and I don't remember much after that—except to say, with a cranial shudder, that they have the most complex flavor perceptible by the human tongue. The region's sole product of interest, these brain-food items make the best Falernian, vintaged under the timeliest frost ever to settle on Campania, taste like lukewarm whey by comparison.

Normally, of course, potential poison-tasting would be the slave's function. But in this case it seemed pointless, if not sacrilegious, to waste the mushrooms' magical effects on Graptus' mind, so to speak. An unfree consciousness is, by definition, rudimentary at best, and probably spends most of its non-drudging time awash in the demon-swarming stupor we free men can only approximate briefly by seeking out and consuming such intoxicants.

So don't expect to hear anything more from me about the details of the close-cropped witch's exit from the earth. This is not to say I recall nothing about that day on the wrong side of the Adriatic. I retain more inside my head than any socialized person would want festering there. But, thanks to the naughty little scamps with the white-spotted red caps, my memory's version of the hag's tonsure holds together about as well as our poor boat did, once Graptus loaded it with us and Great Auntie's pelt—which, it only now occurs to me, might have been cursed. Supernatural agency could explain the inexplicable way the planks went all flaccid and melted under us.

Spado's our touring troupe's expert on spiritual matters, and he's certainly aware of any curses he might be toting around like a sun-bonnet. But my traveling companion doesn't care one way or the other, and it's easy to see why not. The most potent and bitter hex must bounce like a mud-minnow off such a cetacean vitality. I am safer wrapped around my obese eunuch than I would be tucked amidships on a mighty grain freighter, Ostia-bound in perfect weather.

Speaking of seagoing vessels, one of our boat's flaccid, melted planks happened to slosh into my peripheral vision at this very moment. This bit of wooden business floated up, softly enough to slide under Spado's attention, and came into contact with me. Actually, it might not have been a plank. Rather a gloppy thing, identifiable only, and just barely, as some sort of residue of our previous circumstances. If it was wooden, its splinters seemed awfully spongy, and even appeared to writhe a bit—which wouldn't be surprising if I hadn't lost the mushrooms. Seesawing on the miniature wavelets that pass for tides on becalmed Adriatic days, this unspecifiable mass started tapping me on the shoulder.

"Goodness gracious," Spado was warbling, still oblivious. "I do feel a bit peckish between the ear-holes. Unwedge the mushy-jar from whatever orifice in which you've so cleverly concealed it, Aceronia. Break the special elm-sap seal, and dip your petite paw into the luxuriant bee jism." He caressed me with, I think, unfaked affection.

My eyes began to unload their own small barrels of salt water. I must do penance for breaking such a big, soft heart as this dear castrato's. I must atone for losing our only provision and provender, purchased with the murder of a human being, sort of. But make no mistake: my tearfulness was the strong, silent type, and no flighty mood shift befitting a eunuch. No womanishness was in play here, I assure you. I am no pathic swathed in transparent gauze of Tyrian purple, who craves the mollification of rectal intercourse late at night on the Rostrum in the Forum, back home, within the gates of the beloved city of my despicable nativity. Spado didn't even know I was sad. (Though, admittedly, that doesn't say much: as you may have noticed, he's the most self-absorbed biped ever to make do without feathers.) No, in fact, my tears expressed proper manly bereavement.

Without realizing it, I began to lament out loud: "Oh, why couldn't we have lost Gr'Auntie's effeminate scalp and saved her nutritious, wholesome mushrooms, instead?"

"Excuse me, honey? I didn't quite catch that. You need to hack the kelp from your craw before orating. Or whatever it is you're attempting so adorably to do. I hope you're not talking to yourself already. There will be plenty of time for delirium once our bodies realize there's no potable water in our future."

As I tried to get on with my self-mortification, that unspecifiable memento of our dead boat, that spongy, writhing plank or whatever it was, kept hanging about and distracting me, smearing glops of its gloppy self on me, tapping me irritatingly on the shoulder. Its nudges maintained a strangely familiar rhythm, an intimate tempo which one would not associate the currents and tides in this strip of sea between home and the bad place. The flotsam's importunate tapping seemed more in synchronization with the timing of one's personal microcosm than with the planetary pulse. It was almost as if the accidental wad of wood, or protoplasm, was actuated by something riding on top of it, or snagged within it, as if some more or less sentient being with a heart—albeit an undersized, malformed one—was deliberately rocking this dead baby boat, and making it bop over and over again against the bone of my bony shoulder.

I wished it would stop, but feared to relinquish my handholds to push it away. I considered blowing bubbles at the undulating mess, but that would involve putting my lips into the crumby, reeking froth it exuded. Spado could make it disappear, no doubt, with a single glare of the eyes. Sun on mildew. But something told me not to call his attention to it.

Our former boat, or any constituent particle thereof, could have been foundering in the Milky Way, as far as my traveling companion was concerned. Well-padded, he felt no taps, no nudges—nothing but my fingers, to which he responded by caressing me some more and cooing, "See to the jar business, won't you? My mouth waters, my brain waters. Certain other bits of dear

27

old Momsy aren't exactly parched, either, as you can tell with that impertinent little kneecap of yours."

I pulled my leg away in embarrassment.

"I'm thinking of banishing Graptus back across the Adriatic," he murmured, with characteristic absentmindedness. "Sluggish boy can't even keep pace when we're on our way to wherever murdered Queen Dowagers and their pissy entourages go. Don't ask me, I'm just a priest. Maybe the underworld—or, as I've taught Graptus to call it, the *after*world. That fine distinction makes him slightly less mopey about wasting his existence catching my farts. Anyway, fuck him. I know I did. *'shroom* time!"

The whole miniature flotilla came unfocused behind my penitent tears. Not even a shipwreck violent as the one that dumped Aeneas in Dido's lap could excuse such slovenly carelessness as mine. Spado's brains, not to mention mine, were doomed to die of malnutrition, thanks to me. There was nothing else to do but break the sappy seal of my person, to open my throat like a throw-away container, to take in a fatal draught of the poison sea, to slurp the bile-green amniotic syrup that had become our nauseous element. I let go of Spado's muscles, just as I had let go of a jar of similar hardness, and was consigning my contemptible, irresponsible, womanish self to the finny deeps—when, to my surprise, the Priest of the Ineffable Goddess grabbed me by one ear. It was like a reversal of the process splinter-Jews can be seen subjecting each other to in drainage ponds. He pulled me back up into the airy part of creation, at least as far as the nostrils and mouth. Evidently, Spado would rather not drift in perpetuity without my company.

"What's your name again, sweetie?"

"Aceronia?"

"No, that's not it. Really?"

It wasn't only the inlets and outlets of my breath that got raised up. My heart did, too. Even if you're a staid relic-Republican like me, you must find it heartening when a distinguished member of the Ineffable Goddess' Blessed Priesthood spares one of his gesticulating arms to anchor your spares one of his gesticulating arms to anchor your drowning spirit to his unsinkable body. When he delivers you from death, ransoms you, affords you salvation, diverts you from self-slaughter, this holy man—rather, holy *person*—grants you the boon of your life. Like a castrato carved of cork, blissful redemption broke the surface of my sadness and began to bob up and down in the bright turquoise air. An assassin's oar can only glance off a head happy as mine.

"Yes," I said, once I caught my breath. "Aceronia. I think. I don't know."

The Ineffable Goddess' glorious gelding chucked me under the chin. "What a whimsical name for a loyal brave dowdy twat with a paddly-waddly planted square in the middle of her low-slung dishwater-blond monkey brow—*ooh!*" He squeezed me till I squeaked like a monkey. "Ah, me! So sad! Won't the Shaker of the Earth rise from the muddy bottom and save this wretch who suckles and tickles at my ample dugs—which, I see, have already turned red and sprouted white spots and assumed a definite toadstool shape. *Hint-hint*."

Spado wiped away my tears with an elbow-sized knuckle, enabling me to focus somewhat more sharply on the jetsam sloshing against my shoulder. My blissful redemption turned out not to be a castrato carved of cork, after all. It was a round, hard, shiny artefact, molded of clay, glazed and kilned. Heaving into sight as if on cue, balanced fortuitously on that disintegrated slice of witch-blasted boat, shining in the sun like an hallucination engendered by the ingestion of its contents, intact, elm-sap seal unbroken, it was, by coincidence that could only be providential, none other than the very container whose loss I'd been mourning. It was as if a proper sea nymph had rescued our snacks and fetched them here, safe and sealed, to serve us well. I could hear the mycoid chorus chanting profundities within.

"Let's turn into a couple trans-Adriatic fruiting bodies," said Spado. "Talk about the bearing of spores. I'm ready for my snacky-poo now!"

There was something in tow behind the jar—something hardly describable, except, perhaps, by the vague modifier *off-putting*. Snagged and dragging along in the saline muck of the plank's wake was this sort of semi-entity, or maybe just a slick of diluted red grease endowed with a minimal amount of animation. A few fibers of its red hempen rags had gotten tangled in the broken bits of wood. If alive, this red raggedy thing was only half-heartedly so. It smelled like death, but an inconsequential one, and it made sounds that seemed imploring and pathetic. I decided to deal with it later. Now to think only of sea nymphs, not the death-smelly Cyclopses who ride them from behind. Now to ride my warm wave till it curled and broke all over a blissful beach.

Spado was too busy feigning Empress Momsyhood to notice the miraculous recovery of sweetness-swimming salvation. He chortled up and down three octaves. "I'm so jealous, because my beefy mitt won't fit. You must reach in and hand-feed me, like a lynx in the municipal menagerie."

My traveling companion was using only one arm for cleaving the waves, gesturing obscenely at Jupiter, fondling his spit curls, and achieving various other rhetorical effects. His other arm was wrapped around my shoulder. This freed my own hands to turn loose of their muscle-holds—I mean, with non-suicidal intentions. If I happened to feel like it, I could deal with the special elm-sap seals on any jars that happened to be navigating in the vicinity.

"Don't let me grow impatient, now, dearie. You know how fretful and pettish I get when my wants are not gratified instantaneously. I get all pouty, like *this*. Sometimes I even slap!"

Here I must confess to succumbing to a couple of the most un-stoical impulses: gluttony and furtiveness. Without the obese eunuch noticing (his eyes were closed in the performer's rapture), I wiped a few gouts and shreds of what appeared to be someone's small intestine from the rim of the jar, and cracked the seal (not listening to the red tangled thing, whose moans were starting to sound like the words *master* and/or *mistress*, uttered in a plaintive tone).

Maybe it was due to the emptiness of my stomach, but before I even reached into the stickiness, just on the strength of the escaping vapors that hit my nostrils, the sea suddenly became clear as Alpine air in the month of May. The Adriatic jiggled once, like aspic in a shallow bowl, and vanished to the eyesight. I'd eaten nothing so far, yet already we were hanging in hallucinated nothingness. I could, without my wonted squint, catalogue each pebble beneath us, and count every pulsating phosphorescent chartreuse starfish, way down there on the crystalline bottom. Our two pairs of feet dangled miles and miles over copulating eels and burping sea slugs—which added vertigo to my horror. With one or two very minor alterations, that vertiginous horror was transmogrified into delight.

Just as I was about to fetch my spore-bearing snack, a cloud of a familiar color rolled in and obscured my sea-bottom panorama. As if to compensate for the sky's utter decongestion, this opaque cloud billowed up between my legs, around my navel, up under my chin, and into my awe-gaping mouth, where it registered a rusty taste, like gore shed in heavy-breathing panic. Seeming to originate from the environs of the broken board, or whatever that mess was behind it, the cloud sloshed into the tight space between me and the obese eunuch, and lathered the pair of us with slippery, gritty red froth. I heard myself murmur, "And here I thought Nero's momsy was post-menopausal."

"Hmm? What are you babbling about now? Somebody's ragging *mater*?" The eunuch's obesity began to increase, the volume of his voice to swell. "I am the most reverend and sacrosanct *she!*"

Something told me to focus, again, on the amorphous item. It floundered on one side like a sardine in Naples Bay, hooked but not reeled because the angler has been brained by a flying tumor puked from Vesuvius' inflamed craw. The thing twitched and bubbled. Something puckered, crumbly, curled-up and half-hatched

31

about this floater put me in mind of uterine detritus sloughed from overbearing females: fetuses in varying stages of non-viability; Illyrian tykes infected with honeycomb disease, glopped in layers on the raunchy forest floor. That series of notions—or maybe it was more of a single sensation, a fish nuzzling up the spine—seemed to communicate itself to Spado by osmosis. Maternity's moister aspects slipped into his speech, as he continued to grow fatter, taller and louder.

"I am," he intoned, "the magnificent creature who grunted and shat her own murderer from between lubricated thighs!"

Time for a certain someone to dig in. Honey lubricated my fist all the way up to the knobby wrist bone, and I gorged way more than my allotted single one of the numinous tidbits. I clamped jaws upon the endometria of the forest floor, mushy and crunchy at the same time. The complex fungal bouquet was complemented in a most gourmetic way by the dying smell that steamed behind the plank. It was as if the thing crumpled among the splinters had also sprung from the rot of the squalid trans-Adriatic dirt, a twin parasitic growth upon Illyrian decay, the same species as the vegetative growth that I was destroying with my mouth, a nephew to this red-headed auntie.

The redness, not to mention the raggediness, was registering upon my nose with increasing recognizability, and upon my ears with growing intelligibility. Its moans were taking the rudimentary shape of something like childish sentence fragments. Again I heard both the masculine and feminine forms of the M-word, used interchangeably, or maybe just confusedly.

The expanding momsy of Nero was ranting in crescendo: "And don't think I rejoice in having neglected to strangle my matricidal bastard with these strapping labia majora when I had the chance!"

The major lips in question contracted in rhythm, impressively, on the word *strangle*. I felt them through the gore-fecundated brine. Good enunciation. Fine embouchure.

Amazing muscle control where no muscles, no tissue at all, properly speaking, existed.

For this account to remain rigorous, I should pause a moment here before I actually swallow, and make it clear to you that the "vulva" Spado boasted and cherished and cultivated between his elephantine thighs was rather a mass of scar tissue, arranged with moderate Greekling surgical skill around a urinary meatus slightly more cavernous than average for a freeborn Italian. I know this only because we travel together. Spado fondly referred to this idiosyncrasy as his "cicatrice" when not moaning about it constituting his "mons veneris."

With my mind I knew this. But, with my kneecap, I felt something else: a contradiction, a nay-saying, of Mother's words. It was neither cicatrice nor vaginal vestibule. My knee was jammed reluctantly against the undulating organ, and I sensed it to be that other hole-shaped thing, that fanged vacancy, which your big momsy possesses and controls.

It started belching—not farting, but *burping*—planet-sized bubbles of womb gas that enveloped my head and popped, first with snickers, then growls, then gnashing sounds that only gradually evolved into language.

"Oh, what could have been preoccupying my mind at the time?" it cried. "Why didn't I squinch up my quim-sphincter as the Divine Empress Mother-Fucker broke surface and came squawking up for air? Why didn't I bite off his spotty red head? Think how different the history of the stupid barfing Roman cock-wipe Empire would be, if not for old Agrippina's lack of forethought!"

My kneecap was bopping against teeth down there. And they weren't those of the dreaded vagina dentata. No, it was proper oral dentition. The mouth itself had undergone displacement. And its bubbles, when they popped, released the reek of tooth decay, fetid roots seeping deep into the pelvic jawbone. It put me in mind of patrician gourmets and their fondness for a hint of corruption in their supper.

A decadent habitue of the Palatine with two and a half molars, shiny-black, rattling around and festering nicely in his jaded head, savors what these stumps can lend to, say, live baby meadowlarks. When he bites down at just the correct angle they release, sauce-wise, a modicum of the liquescent exudations of the nerve that languishes within his root canals. His enamel has flaked away, his quick is exposed to the light of day, his most intimate pulp throbs.

The point at which the caries seeps all the way down into the vital nerve: that's where you begin to achieve the more complex bouquets that sometimes require eight or ten heartbeats to register fully upon the palate. And you do count the heartbeats, for each is a throb of agony. And agony, of course, is the most piquant spice of all—just ask the better sort, our Senatorial and Equestrian classes. No gravy contrived by human hands can compete. Chomped upon with the proper amount of vigor, a doomed bicuspid smells just like the scarlet mess snagged to the back of our dead boat's plank, or one of these red and white Queens of Mushroom Land, with their most complex flavor perceptible by the human *etcetera*.

And yet, was this aroma necessarily of teeth? Could it be simmering from any other type of liquefying human tissue? Maybe it wasn't coming from Spado's pussy-tusks after all, but from the red membranes of fizz that crackled on the surface of that moaning, mumbling raggedy thing. It was not merely tapping now, but clutching at my shoulder and murmuring intelligibly in my ear.

It twitched in misery, seeming to say *ouch* over and over again. Yet so inveterate were the timed throbs, they lulled the sufferer to drowsiness by the monotonous indications of its own heart's not being quite dead yet. I could feel its rhythmic wavelets lap lazily against my shoulder, tapping, clutching. I looked close and saw more or less hard whiteness among the red. Was it maybe not a mess of pulsating teeth, but a rack of ribs splintering from a shattered sternum?

The sight made me gag, not altogether unpleasantly. The mushrooms with their honey chaser hit the bottom of my stomach and bounced back up to the top of my head via the sinus passages. Servile blood mixed with fish shit and blended with squid piss, plus imaginary imperial birth gore, and that complex sauce engendered an apparition.

I don't know if she's in Spado's repertoire of female impersonations (I doubt it), but haunting the forests of Illyria there is a deformed demoness. Her torso doubles as her face, for she has no head upon which to wedge a wig. Terrifying to relate, her nipples are eyes, her navel a nose, her urinary meatus a most vulgar and halitotic mouth. If Spado was impersonating this barbarous grotesquery rather than Agrippina or Semiramis or Medea or Messalina, I would've been using his earlobes as handholds.

Demonic possession had occurred, let there be no doubt. The witch whom we thought we'd left behind crownless in the Illyrian dump had returned in her true astral form, wanting her sunset-colored coiffure back. She gritted and clamped her fangs on my knee and breathed Spado's nether-voice in my ear, and chanted—

"And who is my murderer, whom I birthed but forgot to cunt-throttle? Who owes existence to my killed carcass? Who kills his mistress? The derelict slave, that's who! Who immolates Mama? The bad boy! That is who!"

Canines, bicuspids, incisors, hemorrhaging gums—I was wrapped around a demoniac, an energumen, a headless gorgon. I gasped air and gulped water till my skull filled with delirium's gritty effervescence. I was making like a barnacle or limpet on no faux-deified Empress Mother, nor any other heavenly woman. I clung to a more infernal type of female, a demoness. It was the torso, which was also, monstrously, the face, of the acephalic bugaboo. It was her ears I held in my hands, and they were situated where armpits are normally found.

"Who," she twat-flatulated, "is my murderer's inferior little brother? What lazy tardy boy dragged behind his pushier twin, so wound up neck-wrung at parturition by Mama's killer-whale snatch? What laggard got undone at the precise moment of coming into being? Who is the partial-birth abortion, the mismanaged miscarriage, the botched butt-plug boo-boo baby? Who comes back now from the fetal dead to avenge himself on me by breaking my heart with his tardiness, and sloth, and deficit of solicitude, and lackadaisiality, and slipshod approach to the art of valeting? Who hankers to kill me with neglect? Who is the servant who murders the mistress? Who is Nero's identical twin?"

Cue Graptus. With tardiness typical of a living chattel in his price range, he made his entrance. Spado's drudge, long-suffering (but probably not much longer) had caught up with us on some random, small current. He was riding in on the same flotsam as our brain fodder, dragging along behind, splinter-snagged. Those opaque billows were oozing from his meager belly.

The inferior Illyrian did his substandard best to report for duty. But he was unable to muster the wherewithal to produce more than a hoarse whisper from what appeared, to my honeyed eyes, to be lacerated lungs strained through collapsed ribs. Whatever excuse he had for gross dereliction of duty was drowned out by his master's transgendered strutting and fretting.

"I'm here, Mistress," sputtered Graptus, almost in a whisper, but not quite. "I had some trouble, but I am here now. I bring—" He couldn't bring that last sentence to full period for lack of puff.

It was impossible to tell if Spado really didn't notice the third party newly come amongst us, or if he was just postponing acknowledgment as a form of torture. In much the same way a mother will ignore a tyke who wants to play or shit or something. Bobbing like a soggy cork this edematous steer might have been, but he towered over us in the water, his gaze fixed on the heavens, as befits a priest and/or priestess. It would have been easy for him to ignore, or feign to ignore, the miserable splorts and splashes of us mere pair of grease spots down here on the darkened surface.

"Master, I did work. You didn't have to tell me or beat me. I did work all by myself."

"Too bad Graptus-*craptus* couldn't be bothered to join me," sneered Spado, preening himself in the sunbeams which his bulk eclipsed from our heads. "Here I am, encased in a sunlit womb, a dream of weightlessness and comfiness in balmy bath water, drifting along. Graptus would enjoy this. I wouldn't have the heart to tell him it's only the first leg of our retrograde journey into featureless *death*!"

Graptus flinched at that syllable. It took every bit of his strength, but he managed to squeeze out a pretty respectable flinch. The water got redder and lumpier, so I reckon that's not all he squeezed out.

The only acknowledgment of the slave's arrival on the shores of our portable archipelago was no acknowledgment of him at all, but of the jar. Spado reached down and poked an index finger in (that's all he could fit). Then he found some rhetorical excuse to gesticulate broadly with that finger, aspersing Graptus with a splash of the daisy-colored sweetness. This, on the surface, might appear to be some sort of liturgical boon, a blessing peculiar to the practitioners of this Ineffable Goddess cult. But quite the contrary. If deliberate, it was an act of exquisite cruelty.

Graptus cringed at the honey even more violently than he did at the D-word. The mere suggestion of bees was a torment for him. Being Illyrian by birth and therefore reared in filth, he had chronic terminal eczema all over his body. He found the bare thought of any bug hideous, productive of squirms and moans—for his skin disorder had infiltrated and suffused his sensorium. Bee stings and their accompanying venom set his teeth less on edge than just the naked notion of the bristles on their legs and the minuscule fuzz on their abdomens, coated with the Ineffable Goddess only knows what gritty pollens.

On our travels he would shudder and swoon and vomit when we passed by any example of porousness, say a volcanic rock face, or dried split pomegranates under a tree. Any repeated pattern of holes reminded him of his own skin pores, which had, since babyhood, tortured him with non-stop itchiness. The honey with which his master anointed him might as well have been the aconite Nero persuades his political enemies to drink, by way of state-imposed suicide. The main difference is that aconite corrodes from the inside out, instead of vice-versa.

Graptus was more appalled at having to share a life raft with a jar of that particular stuff than he was at having suffered whatever trauma caused his own darker leakage. And it was a measure of this slave's pathetic eagerness to serve, to please, to be loved, that he had laid hands on a container full of the irritant, scrounged for it a relatively buoyant conveyance, and dog-paddled it to his owner, no doubt suffering barely supportable pain with each stroke. It was fascinating to try to imagine how the salt crystals suspended in the sea must've been abrading against the raw rim of his open wound—for that was the source of the discoloration of the sea all around us.

"I fetched your special sweeties, Mistress. I dove for them. I saved them."

No reply.

"Master, the birds are flying that way. We should follow them to land."

"Spado, he says something about birds."

"Who? I hear and see nobody but myself. And maybe you. In any case—"

"Please don't ignore me, Mistress. I can't be dead yet."

"—anyone talking about birds under these circumstances is an ignorant, silly boy. A stupid, stupid, lazy, *tardy* boy, who doesn't know a thing about seamanship or nautical, um, techniques. Solidity is right over there. A perfectly serviceable land mass is so close that we free-born humans, whose ears are not tamped with scratchy bits of nauseating beeswax, can hear the grains of sand abrading against each other whenever a puff of wind causes a tiny ripple at the shoreline. Are the tardy farty boy's ears stopped? Can't he hear pebbles and shells and bits of coral grit abrading yonder strand, scrubbing the shingle, like a world-wide skin rash that will never, *ever* go away, not as long as existence itself obtains in the universe? What sort of miserable itchy-flaky-scabby drudge boy would fail to notice such obviousness? Well, I'll tell you what sort. Only a member of the sickliest generation of Illyrians ever sold."

Spado slipped into his confidential mode, which constituted an ear-splitting whisper and a rumbling roll of his boulder-sized eyes. "You know, Aceronia," he said, "my slave might consider himself to be as important as Nero. An equal. A kind of twin, even. But his socioeconomic background is actually far more sordid and squalid than any member of the Claudian *gens* or Julian tribe, or what-the-fuck-ever. Far from being able to boast the divine Augustus among his forbears, this vermin comes from—"

"Acorn scroungers. I know. Spado, maybe we—"

"And do you know why his generation of dirt-snouters is particularly contemptible?"

"I have heard something about the shading of the garrison in those days," I replied. Far be it from me to pitch in on the slave's torment. But no true Roman can resist the opportunity to display arcane knowledge of our imperialistic accomplishments overseas.

"Yes," I continued, "it's not easy to guess the age of someone so—well, you know. But he could very well have been born, or in the delicate stages of early nurture, around the time our great General Fufius was compelled to shade the Illyrian garrison by a legion or so, and send them out to Armenia to keep an eye on the trousered Parthians. To compensate for the reduced military presence, he encouraged slave traders to cull the Illyrian population as much as they liked."

"Very good. And that is how a miscarriage like *Crapped-us* wound up staining the auction block with leakage from his unbut-tocked—well, no need to be indelicate in our exposition. And, later—"

"Here are your special sweeties, Master. I saved them. Something down there fought me for them. It's still underneath us. We need to go away."

"—*later*, I say, in his so-called 'life,' when he recrossed this sea in attendance upon our party, Graptus had a hand in acquiring my hairpiece. You know all about that, don't you, Aceronia, dear?"

"No. Please. I really don't want—"

"The uncivilized sorceress considered herself something of a priestess, a rival to me—not the most secure position to place herself in. And in that professional capacity she was even more reluctant to part with her jar full of fungal sacrament than with her freckled pate. In spite of her presumed esoteric skills, she wound up more or less dying during the negotiations. Maybe that goes without saying. Can one survive sans padding over the seams where head bones mesh?"

"Elder Pliny nowhere treats of that particular—"

"You might wonder, Aceronia—my love, my number-one favorite member of the royal entourage, whom I esteem infinitely higher than any Illyrian with an icky-*fucky* complexion—how such an insect physique as Graptus' managed to flay a rock-hard witch-skull. Let me tell you, after a little verbal prodding from the boss, he got well into it. Imagine that. His own tribeswoman, the disloyal runt. His own great auntie. But, of course, even while getting moist, he moaned throughout the whole chore, from laziness as much as feigned distaste, for he is the most indolent slave ever to have been abducted as a rickety tot from the ratty forest of Illyria by a myopic merchant and fetched across the drizzly Adriatic in substandard shipping, to be got rid of, cut-rate, on-special, in Rome's most depressing transtibertine district. Graptus is not here to defend himself, of course, and one shouldn't speak ill of the *dead*—"

The unlucky slave gave off another tortured flinch at the D-word, accompanied by a further release of red lumps, and more anguished moans.

"—but unfree creatures don't have the right of self-defense, anyway. Nor any other."

Barely audible to me, elaborately ignored by Spado, Graptus' accounting for himself came dribbling from among the chunky foam: "I saw Gr'Auntie's milk-teats turn to eyes. Her belly-button to a nose. Her lady-hole into a mouth. I saw teeth down there. Mistress, we can't stay here."

"Yes, indeed, *Gr'Auntie*—or some other sort of dickless forbear." Again, Spado started speaking in his own tenor and looking down into my eyes. (Frankly, I prefer his alternative selves. The grand historical ladies are not so, shall we say, unrelievedly uncharitable.) "It's impossible to be more specific than *forbear* with these trans-Adriatic degenerates. They haven't invented the notion of family or marriage yet. They're not even suspicious of where babies come from, assuming they spring spontaneously through an act of will on the part of their slaggy slatterns, who shit them out by the litter. Each semi-solid preemie is botched worse than the elder sibling on whose brittle heels it follows, slopping out in layers upon the infected Illyrian mud."

"I saw terrible teeth down there, in double rows. I took more than Gr'Auntie's hair away with me. Oh, Mistress, I can't be dead yet. I must crave a boon from you first."

Spado didn't hear that, of course. For dramatic contrast, or perhaps as a cruel tease, or just out of boredom, he slipped back into the fond, gruff masculine mode, in which he praised his dead slave in absentia. The effect on Graptus was pathetic. It made him temporarily forget the boon he craved and the body parts he was losing, and literally buoyed him up several fingers' width in his own gore-slick. For the moment, the slave had his own castrato carved in cork for clinging to. It bobbed just out of reach, like a not particularly hungry angler's lure.

"Still and all," said the master, mannishly as possible, "the little scamp did a pretty darn okay job outfitting the old boss with this sporty toupee. Yep. A snug fit. The suction stood up to that darn-blasted shipwreck, and it has remained wedged on this bristly noggin o' mine. My skillful boy tanned the critter's pelt, he did, in a solution of—"

"Spado, spare me. I don't need to know this."

That interruption, which I'm afraid I might have shrieked a bit, gave Spado a start, just enough to slip him out of Tough Daddy mode and back into dicklessness. He continued where he left off.

"—a solution, a *sauce* compounded of the former owner's gray matter minced and blended with first-in-the-morning castrato wee-wee (fresh and warm, from guess who's urinary meatus—*tee-hee!*), plus a careful selection of assorted dog turds. Active ingredient, don't you know. I have no idea where the—let's speak frankly, shall we?—*feeble-minded* drudge learned the recipe. I assume it must be an oral tradition among the illiterate Illyrian head hunters."

"Wait a moment!" I heard myself cry out in protest, without altogether intending to. "Head hunters? You can't be serious. In Illyria? That's just across the Adriatic from—"

"I know, I know. Appalling, isn't it? Do any hyper-extended empires spring to mind that could stand a little ass tightening, administratively speaking? I mean, I'm not naming names, but this is ludicrous, right?"

Then, surprising everyone involved, Graptus managed to tighten his own ass, so to speak. Out of nowhere, he generated enough wind to speak loudly. He had air for only three words, but they could not be ignored.

"Manumit me, Mistress."

Spado's eyes exploded with the most baneful, hateful blast of sheer ire I'd ever seen. The demoness was not acephalic anymore. She had grown a head for no other reason than to house two orbs that might have been called celestial in magnitude, if not for their infernal expression. The obese eunuch was looking, finally, at his hemorrhaging slave.

"What did you say?"

"Don't let me die a slave."

Spado raised his left arm. It sailed high over the sea like a blue whale's mile-long flipper. He was about to deal that single downward swipe, that re-killing chop to the neck, that guaranteed death-blow, flat down across the tentative filaments that looped life so loosely to his slave. Our doldrummed voyage's second tidal wave was in the offing. I just had time to hug the open end of the precious honey jar to my own ribby torso and squeeze it tightly shut, and my eyes, and my nose and mouth.

Graptus was indeed smitten, but not from above. Before Spado could strike his blow, something heaved up underfoot like a vast barfing belly. It scattered us in three different directions.

The heaving belly pushed, harder and harder, till the water I'd come to accept as our terminal element went away. And the sand-belly continued to push up, until my legs were useless under my own weight. Then it hit me square on the jaw.

* * * *

I more or less found myself plopped, cross-legged, slammed on something not too unlike a beach. I was nursing what the slave in his baby-talk had called our "special sweeties." The mouth of the jar was honey-glued to me, but had been able to form only an imperfect seal with the corrugations of my contemptible rib cage. I feared contamination. That's all I could think of: salt adulterating the bouquet.

Graptus languished and spasmed in a reddened tidal pool just next door. Spado held the expiring little body as though it was already dead, striking a pose, as usual. This time he had selected Isis from his repertoire of female impersonations. She was mourning over her defunct son or husband, or both, or whatever. The Egyptians can be difficult to interpret at times.

"So, boy," the eunuch yawned, shaking grit from his bouffant, making sure plenty peppered the exposed mucous membranes that quivered in his lap. "How are you holding up? Do tell me. In *very* general terms."

43

"Thank you for asking, Mistress," came the whisper. "I have felt much, much better in the past. But please don't trouble yourself over me." He tried, but could not prevent himself from hiccoughing up something roughly tubular, semi-solid and blackish-red. There was a web of white tendons at one end.

"Try to contain yourself," quipped Spado. He winked at me, brim-full of warmth and fondness for his own drollery.

Graptus moaned, "Master, you always promised to reveal my origins to me someday before I pass into the afterworld. I fear it's today or a broken promise."

Spado flitted a little smirk in my direction. "Oh, of course. The *after*world!" Out of the side of his mouth, so the boy wouldn't hear, he asked me, rhetorically, "What do the splinter-Jews always say about giving scandal to the little ones?"

Then he dropped a few superficially dutiful words into his lap. "Be comforted, if you must, *Crapped-us*, by the doctrine which I as a priest, have always taught you: the Ineffable Goddess treats the downtrodden with especial sympathy in the—" On the next word Spado barely bothered to suppress a catty snicker. "—*after*world." He followed that up with a jolly elbow in Graptus' gnawed-off ribs, which elicited a sigh of mortality. Or perhaps it was just air escaping from a lung-puncture.

Over the boy's burst belly, Spado rolled his eyes facetiously at Aceronia, me, who was wondering if my skull could hold another fistful of fungus. It wasn't the white-spotted red caps that challenged me, but the honey. The endless sweetness was starting to crystallize at the backs of my eyeballs.

"*Who* promised to reveal your origins to you one day? Are you sure it was me?"

"Before I died."

"Bless my cicatrice if I can recall ever promising that."

"Maybe you had better tell me today, Mistress."

"Nonsense, my boy. One doesn't really need all these pearly-red sausages and things spilling out in such profusion from your, um, thorax. You'll be fit to scout us up some firewood in no

44

time at all. And fetch nasty little nuts and berries, and mutilate any number of helpless elderly ladies."

Then my traveling companion realized that, with this obviously disingenuous death denial, he was missing a marvelous theatrical opportunity. Geldings cannot afford to pass up such chances. Their unfamilied existence denies them unfaked scenes of maudlinity between linked, or maybe just stuck-together, souls. So he shifted positions quickly before this moment could pass—pass *away*, to be more exact.

"Allow me," he said, "to get more comfortable."

He jostled his dimply thighs to a more motherly and mournful attitude, like a bas-relief of Isis cradling her dead male propinquity. Being Egyptian, this posture was stiff and hieratic, and never intended to accommodate traumatized tissue. So the adjustment elicited another release of entrails, and would have raised a scream of distress from the boy, if he'd possessed the strength.

After pondering the small spectacle of an Illyrian fading further, Spado sighed in mild irritation and said, "Oh, all right. I suppose I'm as comfortable as I'm likely to get. I shall now reveal your origins to you."

Hanging halfway off the rim of the abyss nobody has ever described first-hand, Graptus somehow dragged himself back, just a few fingers' width. He opened his entire self, not just his ears and lower abdomen and eyes, but the invisible spirit which he assumed was inside there, not yet slopped out. His master, the priest of the Ineffable Goddess, had never taught Graptus to doubt that spirit's existence and eternality, because it made him more amenable to non-stop grunt work. So the slave laid himself wide, like a fresh wound or a rotten oyster, and craved to have the salt crystals of knowledge rubbed in, the intelligence he'd waited to hear ever since he was able to understand speech. His eagerness for the information Spado had promised to impart was the only thing prolonging the wretched existence that was about to piddle out.

"If you don't calm down and sit still and stop sloshing gore and guts and unshat shit on my mons veneris, I won't tell you a

45

blessed thing," scolded his master, who was on the verge of getting all pettish and pouty. Spado had a tendency to slap people when he got that way.

"I'm sorry, Master," moaned Graptus. "Please, for the Ineffable Goddess' sake, don't punch me."

Spado took a moment to compose himself. His eyes roamed, with mine, the place where we'd landed. Together we were trying to determine which would be the best animal path to trudge inland after this little chore was discharged. Which gap in which pair of rocks seemed to offer the best prospects for the continuation of our journey—if that were not too organized a term to apply to whatever it was we were doing?

The sun hadn't left off laying down its snail-trail of gray snot across the sky, and was going down quickly. So I said, "Before things get really dark, it would be better at least to attain that low rise to get our bearings—to the extent we can get them without the assistance of a certain, as it were, *scout*."

"Shhh! Someone is having himself a moment." Spado indicated *you-know-who* with a subtle downward glance at the mass slopped across his thighs. He looked around a bit and said, "This is a strange place. There are too many different colors of shells."

"I was just going to say that."

Spado began to rock back and forth. Though histrionically justified, the motion caused Graptus to contort in what appeared to be the sort of pure, unimpeded pain that can induce insanity.

In a sing-songy lullaby voice, Spado cooed, "Your momsy was feebleminded. And covered with hair. Red hair. And so bestial that people decided to place her in the pen among the offerings to the fanged infernal deity to whom pregnant victims are sacrificed in your barbarous slough of a parturition pit. And, just as they cracked her skull with one of the crude rocks your people call implements, you came squirting out (not from her skull—don't flatter yourself): a flop, an unfunny joke, to be cast outside the wattle and daub your people call walls, exposed to the elements on an unsightly hillside, where you were tripped over by a trafficker in so-called 'humans' who was too unscrupulous to balk at dealing in tainted goods. And he unloaded you on my, er, *mother*—"

Spado urped, gagged, and nearly threw up on that particular instance of the ever-loaded *M*-word. It might be interesting to try to bring him out on the topic. Maybe some day when my own stomach is feeling less queasy.

"—who must have been drunk and mad with advanced venereal disease at the time. And we raised you as a household pet for me. Your trifling incarnation was consecrated to my service, as my valet and plaything and punching bag. Also butt-boy—I mean, before my consecration, alteration and ordination into the priesthood. And then you got bitten by a fish or a witch or something. And that's about it."

The look on Graptus' undersized face revealed not so much shock, disbelief and dismay as disappointment. But it was a letting-down so accustomed, so inveterate, as to cause no change at all. So what? Another empty bucket that needs filling, only to be poured out. Another mess that needs to be brought to Master's lips, only to be shat out the other end. Graptus was able barely to mouth his gratitude.

"Thank you."

"You're welcome—" Spado waited one heartbeat. "*Birth-day*-boy."

Those words sent a shudder up the wrecked body. The accompanying pain brought sharpness to Graptus' mind, and he was able to respond in a normal voice, almost.

"Today's my—?"

"What did I just say?"

"So I am of age! I'm finally fit to render my gender to the Ineffable Goddess!"

"Oh, that's *ri-i-i-ight*. I completely forgot about that. My word, you are in a predicament, aren't you? Your future in the *after*world hangs in the balance. Or, rather, in your scrotal sac."

"Please, Mistress, my hands lack an implement, my arms the strength. While there is still time, gather a shattered shell and deballock me now!"

"Oooh, no!" shrieked Spado, shoving him away. It was necessary for the eunuch to shove several times to get all the bits scooped off. Graptus' eczema got coated with grit and pebbles at his mistress' feet. His boss screeched, "Distasteful pecker-snot! Thinking of your private parts at a time like this! Shameless! Besides, do you see any shattered shells within arm's reach?"

"Then smash that jar which your favorite companion cradles so protectively, and use a shard, in the orthodox Anatolian manner, to consecrate me now."

We both yelled "Oooh, no!" this time. With my torso I shielded our supply of honeyed heaven.

"Don't force me to make like a Larissan beaver," said Graptus.

I looked up and asked his master, "What in Hermes' name is that supposed to mean?"

"You don't want to know."

I said, "Yes, I do," and he told me.

"Then please," wept Graptus, "keep your other promise, that I may die free. Manumit me, Master."

Those words sat no better this time than before. Spado raised his whale flipper again. But something, I'll never know what, stayed his hand. Somewhere inside himself Spado found a vein of patience, never before tapped. Sinews and arteries popping from his neck and temples, with effort he lowered his arm and, rather than punching and beleaguering the slave (which would have been no less messy than fatal), Spado spoke, quietly and slowly, through gritted teeth. This was indeed a special occasion.

"If you'll pay attention to something else besides your genitalic urges of the moment, if you'll use your neck muscles to raise your head and swivel it around a bit before the sun goes completely down, maybe you'll notice, Graptus, that we are seated on uncharted territory. Do you see any municipality? Any magistrate?

We lack the legal apparatus to effect such a complex transaction as manumission. And, in any case, I don't suppose you've troubled yourself, over the decades of our association, to sock away a copper here and there, to accumulate by steady thrift and industry your *peculium*, by which you might honestly purchase that boon you now beg from me as a gratuity. You expect someone else to take up your slack. Typical of an unfree morality. Don't you see how presumptuous your request is? Aren't you ashamed?"

"But I've slaved since before I can recall. I feel it's time to—"

"Just now, Graptus, I don't seem to have the price of your liberation tax on me." Spado took a supercilious moment to pat pockets he didn't have, and to heft an absent purse. "And what is five percent of your value? I suppose you have the sum all calculated and counted and secreted about your, um, person. What's left of it. I recall teaching you percentages in avoirdupois and coin before you were out of long hair. You've retained that lesson, I presume. Shall I quiz you on it now?"

I heard someone shout (it turned out to be me), "Spado!"

The possessor of that odd moniker started. He looked into the honey-crusted depths of my eyeballs, where something like disapproval could probably just be descried. He said, "What?" and checked himself for bits of hanging nasal dirt.

"A little—" I paused to burp some fungus up into the basement of my sinus passage, where it promised to impart a special wisdom. "—um, a little *fellow feeling* is called for in this situation. Don't you think? Sort of?"

"Fellow—?"

Spado paused in unfeigned puzzlement. For a moment his big round face looked as it must have long, long ago, before all the multiple shams and interlocking deceits piled upon it—probably just before the crown of his placenta-cowled noggin cleared his unimaginable, sick-making mother's dilated horror.

He said, "I cannot begin to guess what you're babbling about. Maybe a certain lady-in-waiting would do well to go a little

49

easier on the mushrooms. And, rather than interrupting us with non-sequiturs, she might consider condoling with me on my bereavement. I pretty near reared this dead youngster here. Consider yourself chastised, Aceronia. Anyway, Graptus, where were we? Here I am paying attention to your rival in my affections, when this is *your* great big special hoo-ray moment. How I do go on! So, what's on your mind? So to speak."

Graptus separated his jaws, only to be interrupted.

"Fellow-*feeling*?" Spado turned back to me. "I thought all those stoical heroes of yours preached contempt for death. Well, look around. Who's the most contemptible member of this trio? Fellow-*fellatio* is more like it. I'm sorry, Graptus. I had to dispose of your sister's argument with great rhetorical skill. What you just witnessed was a devastating reference to Greekling philosophy, which has left the little bitch speechless, sans rebuttal. So, anyway, please do continue, my stout lad, with—whatever."

"Don't let me die a slave."

"Oh, that's right. The manumission farce. I can tell from the expression on your unhappy face, or rather from certain undertones beneath the chronic affliction, that you consider me yet to be in moral arrears to you. You expect me to pull some priestcraft and make it all better. So now you would be my freedman, my client. And I suppose, as my freedman you'll want to claim your right of appeal to Nero next time I decide to have you crucified."

Snorting with disdain, Spado said to me, "These unfree types, mystifyingly enough, love to breathe. They prefer twenty or thirty years on the wet stones of the Emperor's holding cells awaiting the hearing of their appeal, to the clean, quick death that a day or two on a gibbet affords. I keep telling this scatterbrained child that the crows will get his eyes immediately, so at least he won't have to watch himself die. Am I right in this, or not? What are your feelings?"

"Elder Pliny does say something about crows and crucifixions, but I can't recite you chapter and verse just now. I'm checking our honey jar for cracks, our honey for sea water seepage. Salt may actually enhance mushrooms' potency."

"Yes, well, um—thank you for that, Aceronia. Graptus, my deformed rodent freedman. I suppose you'll want to adopt my surname in the underworld and expect me to take it as a compliment."

"*Under*world? But, Master, the Ineffable Goddess teaches us that—"

I won't say that Spado exactly savored the appalled look that hemorrhaged now from the dying face. Perhaps he just ignored the boy's new grimace of horror. At all events, just for fun, merely to beguile the while, out of boredom, this Priest of the Ineffable Goddess now proceeded methodically to pooh-pooh every tenet of the salvationist creed he'd taught Graptus to build his whole wretched life's hopes upon, from earliest boyhood till now.

But first, in order to achieve the full effect on Graptus' mind, and to give himself maximum enjoyment, Spado consented to gather the eczematous boy back up from the endless itching powder that constituted the shingle upon which he had been shoved and scooped, and to resume the stylized mourning Isis posture. It would probably have been better for the structural integrity of the slave's skeleton and connective tissues to leave him on the ground.

"I exaggerated a moment ago about you being fit to fetch berries and firewood soon. I cannot lie to you any longer, Graptus. I very nearly birthed you, and owe it to you to be truthful."

As the boy was afraid to look down and see for himself, Spado began thus, by way of description: "Your belly bears a scalloped series of indentations. These, taken in combination with the single serrated triangular tooth sloughed off and lodged between your exposed breastbone and a rib—here, hold still, let me dig it out and show you—lead me to deduce that you, my boy, have been chewed. For example, has the ghost of a certain witchy great auntie been at your tummy? Perhaps you were bitten by a large vindictive fish, such as one of those stupid bestial dolphins with the hardly attractive forehead pussies."

51

To me he remarked, with complacency, "It's a question of not merely jeering at the disintegration of the body, but of embracing it, and exploring its esthetic subtleties. Watch this—" Not quite gingerly enough to suit the slave, Spado's gigantic fingers poked about.

"Yes, you are dying, Graptus. No doubt about it. That is my gnosis and my diagnosis. In my quality as your superior and advisor in the Ineffable Goddess priesthood, I should suggest you spit into your bosom for good luck, according to the most ancient usage. But, er, well—" Spado waved a forlorn hand over the absent bosom. "You have nowhere to spit. You really are about to leave not just your body—you'd probably be glad to have done with such a shambles anyway, at this point. It must really *hurt*—" Spado poked around a bit more. "—but you are also about to lose your awareness, permanently.

"I know all those things which the Ineffable Goddess teaches us about the immortality and salvageability of the soul." Spado eyed the seascape wistfully. "And I know this is not the very best time or place to introduce skeptical notions." He chuckled with affection at his own charmingly poor sense of timing. "But, Graptus, even a full-fledged priest like me—such as you wanted to be one day, but never will, because, as you may have already guessed, I was exaggerating about the disutility of these tubes and glops of *you*, drying and puckering and stinking on the itchy sand—even a full initiate into the complete mysteries like myself has moments of doubt. Moments when the sublime comfort of faith wavers, and the rational core of my mind—trained by Greeks, unlike yours, you lucky, naive, ingenious acorn-nigger—demonstrates to me the foolishness of imagining anything more than what my five senses present to me, and doubting even that—"

Spado glanced at me for a gloss, and I said, "That's Pyrrhon. I think. Of Elis. I don't know. These mushrooms are nice with a little saltiness added."

"—but, in any case, suspecting—no, *knowing*, with all my certainty, that this puny awareness of ours is all there is, and death is an extinguishing, and there is nothing left afterwards, not even a lead-gray ghost to stumble around in boring old Hades in numb forgetfulness—no, not even grayness, but blackness, and silence, blacker and quieter than anything you could ever imagine even if you had more than a slave's rudimentary brain—flat lusterless blackness without end, and silence, and numbness."

Graptus somehow found the strength to widen his eyes and tremble, as this idea entered his child-like mind for the very first time.

"It's terrible!" he whispered.

Spado reached down and, sighing, unwedged some shells from the pudge on the downward side of his body, and made it clear—without being rude, of course—that his buttocks would not complain if this business could be concluded sooner rather than later. He shifted around again, with the expected results. The response from his lap was a gurgle of salt water and blood.

"You may well say 'it's terrible.' That's easy enough to say. But do you *know* it's terrible? I want you to take a moment now—though your time be short and your servile mind weak—and really strain yourself to imagine this. I'm talking about complete non-existence. Not 'annihilation' and union with and absorption into some unified force of all life. Not return to the Goddess' Ineffable embrace and her warm creamy knockers with the blue veins. There's no union, no merging. Just—"

"Blackness. Silence."

"Let me finish!" snapped Spado, and beleaguered his cheeky chattel. A slap or two, open-handed, no fists, just light chastisement, but effective under the circumstances. "No, smart-aleck. *Not* blackness." Slap. "*Not* silence." Slap. "Not even those two, since each implies a cessation of the function of a sensory organ. There's nothing to cease. Just nothing. Got that?"

In response, Graptus' trunk turned loose of something greenish that moved all by itself for awhile in a puddle.

53

"I had an excellent friend," said Spado, "a pathic—you may recall him. Name of Old Bofus? He used to come over to the house. He reamed your asshole eight or nine times when you were just a teeny-tiny tot. You probably've forgotten. Anyway, Old Bofus didn't want to live, and was continually attempting self-slaughter by every means imaginable: sword, venesection, defenestration, aconite. And at each crucial juncture, the terrible luck that made him want to commit suicide in the first place would arrange for someone kindly and skilled to happen by and rescue him. Old Bofus was, in fact, a real-life, um—what's the name of that resurrected Greekling-person at Troy?"

"I've forgotten," I said. "I'm worried about salt. Salt's what troubles me. It tastes good, but could alter the mushrooms' medicinal nature."

"Good point, Aceronia, dear. Carry on. What was I just saying? Oh, yes. Old Bofus. He has seen what lies beyond, many times. Each time was the same. And he assures me that it's nothing. No self-conscious attempt at heterodoxy intended, no foolishly brave flouting of the official Greco-Roman statutes against atheism. Merely straight reportage. And that's precisely why Old Bofus will never stop trying until he has attained death. That's just the kind of person he is. A bit tired, I would say. He would envy you now. Personally, I can wait. No hurry for me. But as for you, Graptus, well—oh, wait! Hold on here! Am I making you uncomfortable? Here, let me shift about. Let me raise and lower your head several times in matronly solicitude. Maybe twist your bony shoulders this way. And that. Back and forth. There, is that better? How about now?"

Such loving care came close to killing the injured Illyrian outright.

"You know, I kind of get the feeling you're not entirely thrilled about this idea of nothingness. Well, there's an exception to the rule. Something you do take with you when you go. I don't reckon you want to hear about it."

Graptus would have lurched forward in eagerness if he could.

"All right, then. Do you remember that Hindu longshore-man at Alexandria, the one you scouted for me to blow that muggy night when I felt peckish for a belly full of wog spooge? Well, his people's lawmaker is named Manu, and Manu says words to this effect: *The only thing that follows men after death is justice; for everything else is lost when the body perishes.* Well, Graptus, guess what? You were tardy today. You have served me poorly. You have been a bad, sluggish slave. Justice will follow you. It will eat like eczema into your spirit's epidermis for all eternity. Way to go, fuck-tit."

I looked up from fiddling with a sand crab whose color I could not put a word to, either because I'd never seen that particular hue before or because it was changing all the time, I couldn't say. A tiny place in the pit of my stomach told me to be at least mildly appalled at something or other that was happening nearby. I felt the fungus in my blood form words. Those words, when they came out of my mouth, turned out to be, "Oh come, come. Oh, come. Come. He has served you well enough. Think of the special sweeties he saved. Think of the wig he peeled and tanned. Wipe his brow with your sleeve or something."

Spado shot me the strangest of all the strange glances he has ever shot at me, before or since. The whole mindless progression of the sun was held in abeyance while my attention, the attention of everything, fixed on that gelding's huge face. The saucer-sized eyes focused on me, and the platter-sized mouth said something wordless. It was an invitation to gaze straight down into another human being's brain-hole, past the idiosyncratic and occasional, beyond the rim of individuality, into the crater that encompasses everyone.

Graptus gasped, "But, my Mistress, if the end is so complete, what is the purpose? Is there a point?"

"Purpose? Point?" Spado laughed full out. He jollied and trotted the joker over his fat belly like a galloping mare. "Oh!

Good one, Graptus! The chattel makes a funny! Why didn't you do this more often in life, you wry little bastard? It took you an entire short lifetime, but you finally got a chortle out of Momsy!" Spado slapped him on the shoulder, causing another pale rib to breach the surface of his wound. Seeing this result, Spado slapped him again, with redoubled heartiness. And again.

"It's terrible," repeated Graptus.

"Oh, but I'm frightening you, aren't I? Forget what I just said about perpetual eczema. Never mind. Be consoled instead by the luminous grace of the Ineffable Goddess. May she keep you and console you. May she make the light of her loving face to shine upon you. May she give you respite, amen, and so on and so forth, blah-blah, lick my asshole." The obese eunuch rolled his eyes at me and made a series of mouth farts, wet. "It's such a chore humoring spiritual cowards like grasping Graptus. Our little counseling sessions are hereby suspended *sine die*."

"Mistress, don't let me—"

"Die a slave." Spado gently pushed him into the gentle surf, which sucked his *exta* all the way out, finally. Graptus died with a mouth full of alien salt water, eyeballs abrading under their lids with the sand of an unknown country, to the tune of his mistress trilling a little sing-songy dirge.

"Chitterlings, lights and sweeeeetbreads, *hey!* What would the haruspex make of a liver so uncauled in fat? Would he compliment the master of so wholesome a gland?"

Then my traveling companion came rising up on legs like tree trunks. He brushed bushels of sediment from between his pumiced buttocks and thumbnailed hundreds of clamshells from where they'd snuggled into the dropsied dimples of his titanic thighs. Once de-gritted, he peered into the body of land we had somehow to negotiate. What municipalities, what magistrates lay beyond?

"Now I have no slave to be put to torture on my behalf if I ever go on trial for—"

"For what?"

"Let's just say a potential hostile witness has been removed from my life."

"Slaves' evidence under torture is only heard in incest cases."

"And I have no siblings."

"Yes?"

"I know what you're thinking. No magistrate would credit anybody submitting to intimacies with a specimen like my, ah, *mother*." He gagged, again, on that last word. "And that, my friend, is the only thing I'll ever tell you about the creature as long as you live."

There was utter mortal finality in his tenor voice, accompanied by a sidelong eyelash flutter that said, "I can be persuaded."

Am I curious? I'll have to decide later. A source of potable water is higher on the list of things that must be coaxed from strange mud today. And that chore will fall on—who else?

Nilla-Killa

Little by little, we shall see the universal horror unbend, and then smile upon us...
—Teilhard de Chardin

    Several years back, not by choice, Sam Edwine was living deep in the hinterlands. This locale was so remote that land meant nothing. His neighbor's backyard was big enough for strange people to skulk around in for days and nights on end without being seen.

    Sam's neighbor had sufficient acreage back there, in fact, to accommodate a whole geothermal formation. He proudly called it a "fumarole or a solfatara or somethin'." It was shaped and colored, and even textured, exactly like the lid of a colossal human skull, scalped and trepanned. In the nighttime, peculiar trespassers were drawn like spectral head lice to crawl all over this peeled cranium. They perched on top with butts hanging halfway into the crater, sucking in vapors and communing with whatever invisible chthonians are drawn to such misty apertures under the moon.

    This neighbor did not cut rural Utah's most imposing figure, and he had wisely developed a severe physical cowardice. So he fell into the habit of waking Sam up at two or three a.m. and begging him to chase these weirdos away. Not knowing why, Sam usually surprised himself and complied with the requests. Persuasion was the tool he tried most often on the unwelcome visitors, resorting to violence as little as possible, because he was a nice man, after all, underneath those six feet, nine inches, and three hundred and thirty-seven pounds of orange hair and freckled flesh.

    So, one night Sam awoke to the sight of a head poking into his bedroom window, not two feet from his pillow. Starlight glinted off several buck teeth, and anguish distorted a pair of flaky lips. It was an especially urgent plea this time around.

"He done killed Nilla. An' I don't figger he had oughtn'ter be a-hangin' round my solfatara."

"I thought you said it was a fumarole."

"What-the-damn-ever."

"I see your point. What's a Nilla?"

"Huh?" The little man started to look even more sheepish than usual. "Why, m'third plural wife's half-stepdaughter. Sort of...y'know?"

"Oh, but of course," yawned Sam, broadly and non-judgmentally.

This kindness seemed not to go unappreciated. In spite of the emergency at hand, Sam's neighbor warmed to the conversation. He said, "We used t' call her 'Niller' for short, 'cause vaniller was her fav'rite over to th' soda shop."

Sam started dozing off.

"An' that pot-licker up thar done did her to death. Hey, Big Red? Much obliged if'n you c'd see yer way clear to runnin' him off b'fore Nilly's maw wakes up."

Inspecting the small segment of eastern horizon visible between his neighbor's sloping shoulder and the sash, Sam sighed, "And I'll just bet the farm that Nilly's maw wakes up real early."

"Dang tootin'. She's a early bird. Chores 'n so forth."

So Sam hauled himself out of bed, pulled on some underpants, stepped into his rubber flip-flops, and hulked off into the blackness, to chat up and talk down Niller's Killer. Feeling dutiful and saintly, he labored up the anticline, scraped between some strands of the devil's wire, and approached the crumbling lip of the volcano-hole.

And there, silhouetted against a gritty clot of prune-colored clouds, was (conjecturing from the abhorrence that contorted the rodent-sized sinews in the clean-shaven nape of his neck) not one of Hell's escapees, but their passionate, fanatical enemy. A volunteer sentry, this human tampon stood vigilant at the porous border of our world. He held, in both hands, high over his head, a medium-hefty chunk of calcium carbonate, poised to be chucked deep into Nature's dank outlet, should any questionable entities poke their heads up and bare their fangs.

Being naturally sympathetic to such selfless vocations, Sam decided it would be best if he squatted off to one side, unnoticed, and permitted the unwanted guest to get his rock off before chasing him away.

No harm done. Such a stout little soldier probably had done nothing more sinister than forget to sign his name in an emotionally unbalanced Nillum's high school year book, or neglect to ask her to the big sock hop over at the prayer hall. Most likely something mild like that. Perhaps he'd been a slightly careless young driver, or maybe had once carried "mono," and had known about it, but had refused to quit "makin' out" with a weakly constituted Nillie-kins. Something along those bland lines.

Sam had to admit that he was a bit surprised at the sheer conviction with which this skinny stalwart struck his blow against encroaching damnation. All at once he whinnied and snapped his whole body double like a jackknife, so that for a moment both of his toy-sized feet were off the ground, kicking his palms.

Sam could have told him that excessive zeal is detrimental to marksmanship. The rock didn't even make it into the crater, but sparked off the rim and blasted to bloody atoms a horny toad that was wandering past in search of bugs to eat.

"Missed," observed Sam.

The boy almost leapt into orbit. He twirled around and flashed startled, yet chilly, eyes.

"Missed," Sam repeated, and paused for the polite period of time, to permit a response.

This kid did not seem to possess the ability to make intelligible noises with his mouth, so the conversation was lacking a certain piquancy. It occurred to Sam that his inarticulateness might be caused by paralysis of the lips. Through the darkness, the lower half of that undersized face seemed oddly fixed. For reasons not difficult to pinpoint, suspicions of rigor mortis, of the death rictus, of lock-jawed night-crawling zombies, started to creep up Sam's spine.

But it was such an extra-long spine. While those images were still making their way to his awareness, the moon had plenty of time to rise over the curvature of this vast Death's head, and light up the kid's squinchy kisser. And it was not necessarily with relief that Sam saw what he should have been expecting all along: the Mormon Smile.

It never goes away, this facial expression: the permanently creased gape that in old age curls into a grimace, everlasting as the mint-and-pastel Utah sun grinning down the back of your salty neck in the morning, just spiffy as the reflection off a good Latter-Day-Saint's pearly whites when he's whipping up a breakfast of buckwheat waffles and beaming that fabled Mormon Smile. What it conceals is beyond, or maybe beneath, most non-Utahns' comprehension.

Sam immediately averted his gaze, as Lot's wife should have done. He pretended to inspect his own feet—one of which, to his surprise, had slipped out of its flip-flop and was nervously twitching about in the pale sediment underfoot.

Suddenly, in a single avocado-colored blast, he caught a glimpse of something that caused not only contempt and fear and suspicion, but respiration and heartbeat, to cease. Even the crickets and coyotes took a break. Everything focused down on Sam's big shower flippers.

Way down there, loosening a stain of psychomimetic green onto the aragonite under his grinding heel, just happened to be a bulb full of the concentrated essence of everything potent, grave and reverend yet remaining on the face of this poor depleted Earth. It was the final receptacle for the ghosts of coyote- and iguana-deities, plus Phrygian Cybele and multi-dugged Demeter; the preserver of the souls of prognosticating eunuchs, theriomorphic virgins, and heinous Beelzebub—all chemically wedded within its darling, poison-tufted confines.

A host of these squatty cacti swirled and spiraled around the crater, wherever a teaspoonful of fecund dust had happened to accumulate. Sam had never noticed them before tonight.

"Jesus Mahogany Christ," he whispered, and fell to his naked knees.

The boy did the same. Apparently he thought it a game of Simon Sez; for Sam was forced to lead his bony fingers down to the life forms in question before it dawned on him that the idea was to start gathering them.

And, giggling and salivating in unison, elbows and contrastingly shaped haunches poked high in the air, Nilla-Killa and Samuel Edwine together collected at least a bushel of tomato-sized peyote buttons, plump and succulent as the buttocks of green babies under your arm.

Soon enough, Sam was conducting a stern tutoring session on top of the geothermal formation. Dangling his legs down into the steamy vent, he was showing his new pal how to trepan the asterisks of icky strychnine out of each bulb with a slip of barb wire borrowed from the neighbor's ineffectual fence.

In the presence of this controlled substance Sam began to get all gauzy and sleazy, his lower eyelids pouting like those of a Penthouse model who has, for once, accidentally allowed herself to become aroused in front of that Vaseline-smeared lens. He heard his lubricated mouth going "Mmmmmmm?" with each fomented bulb they sundered and prodded.

Already he felt traces of the sublimity that would descend when they chastised and houseled themselves on the immemorial Uncompahgre sacrament, scarfing this gunk by the sweaty armload. Digesting spineless tubercles was the sole reason Sam Edwine's DNA was braided in his mom's womb in the first place.

So perfectly attuned was he that his tongue became gradually loosened from its frenum. It went into slippery orbit around his cerebral cortex.

"There's no need to fret if your pulp gets stained phosphorescent-orange with oxidation from the devil's wire," mouthed

Sam into the ears of his skinny apprentice, "since I bet iron is one of the nutrients that combat alkaloid poisoning in your system, anyway. And we're bound to miss a few of these lethal angel-hair filaments woven through-and-through the translucent green flesh, the fibrous essence of nux vomica, strung in and out, like systems of unpleasant symbols in an edifying vegetable narrative. Strychnine's what characters in ladies' mysteries murder each other with—

"Oh, and by the way, it makes some guys barf. Never been my particular problem, this barfing, because my whole hefty metabolism was made for these green grapes of insomniac Proserpine. I'm the only person in these parts, besides the Uncompahgre braves themselves, who never even gets a tiny bit queasy. And that fills my favorite homosexual cousin Bryce Barkdull with envy, turning him a visible emerald-green. He speculates that I might have the unfair advantage of some aboriginal blood in my veins, despite my physical type, which, as you can see, m'boy, seems unadulteratedly Celtic—although that doesn't necessarily inspire any undue feelings of narcissism in me. Do you think it should? What's your frank opinion?"

The kid was already looking a tad nauseated, so Sam quickly added, "Just think of the barfing as part of the overall spiritual experience. And try to persuade the greater part of your spiritual barf to slide down into the crater—without falling in yourself, of course. We don't want to lose you at that point, kiddo, because, after the strych doubles you over, the rest of the plant lifts you up and puts a real smile on your little Cupid's bow.

"Meantime, we've got this kitchen chore to do. Let these olive-drab Injun strawberries stain our tootsies, my boy, under the moon, stars and bits of space junk whose reflections obscure them. Fuck my neighbor. Selfish guy thinks a fumarole and its produce can be owned."

It was bound to be true policy Sam talked, for he sat with large portions of his jockey-briefed buttocks flopped over the volcano-hole, in the precise posture of the bare-naked Pythoness at

Delphi, who received divine revelation in the form of magic mineral steam up her oracular snatch. Sam positioned his admittedly vagina-poor crotch in the exact manner his mom had shown him ten years before, when she had taken him on a pilgrimage to the Omphalos. In the dissolving shadow of acid-rainy Parnassus, his bipolar mom had entered into one of her unmedicated manic states, and had demonstrated the proper squatting technique for the Minolta.

And, tonight, here in the New World, Sam began to utter bona-fide doctrine at his fellow harvester (reaper, also, of at least one vanilla soul)—even though the kid was not a particularly good listener, and was starting to exhibit some definite personality problems.

For example, he had already worked himself into such a state of ambiguous agitation that he'd lost all semblance of manual coordination, and was smooshing up his half of the blessed verdure. He just sat there diddling in the dirt with the dope, a juicy finger painting with a street value of seventy bucks, or even seventy-five, depending on whether you could find a high school student to burn. And, in the meantime, he was failing to hold up his end of the social discourse. He just cackled through that ossified grin, and kept muttering "What a brain-fuck!" under his breath, over and over again, regardless of the conversational context.

Even so, despite all this smooshing, diddling, giggling and muttering, Sam had not forgotten the neighborly errand. He wanted to try to address this problematic youth, to exert moral suasion upon him through rhetorical means. Sam would bounce salubrious anecdotes off that petrified facade, like a Hasid bopping the brim of his big hat against what's left of Herod's town hall. Gesturing with a green juice-oozing fist, Sam would feed his junior crater-mate tales of the olden days, the formative years. In the manner of an old salt or staff sergeant, scratching his whiskers and reaching down to adjust his scrotum from time to time, Sam intended to preach.

And it felt very strange, because, search as hard as he might for something sage to say, something big brotherly and uplifting and expressive of regeneration and the sun-also-rising, the only thing he could recall about his youth, under the present circumstances, with those pious Latter-Day-Saint choppers glinting up at him, was a squalid brothel way out in the Salt Flats.

But, what the fuck? We must do the best we can with the materials available to us. So, ignoring the owner/proprietor of this lump of nature, who scampered in tight circles on the dim horizon, trying desperately to catch his eye with one of those "Tell the rascal to skedaddle afore m' third plural wife wakes up 'n poops a peck!" signals, Sam began spinning yarns of the remote epoch when he was hovering at this kid's apparent stage of psychosexual development, during his own drug-drenched teens, in the peak of the High Renaissance.

"Back when I was your age," began Sam—

* * * *

It was an era of enforced liberation, of requisite coolness about Love-Love-Love. All persons under twenty were expected to spend sedate evenings maturely sucking in their pudgy cheeks at "pod-pardies" alongside washboard-tressed, archaically smiling androgynes. Herbal tea was provided to wash down the methaqualone and the artsy-craftsy religion and the Simon and Garfunkle LPs, and every person, regardless of demographics, had an equal right to speak frankly about "balling."

This sort of thing soon wore thin as Joni Mitchell's singing voice, and a certain young Turk began to feel the need for something more substantial. He hankered after crotch-level, butt crack-reeking fun.

So he struck out into the wilderness and linked up with his distant country cousin, one Bryce Barkdull. Resorting to familial blackmail, he held over Bryce's blushing head various whispered secrets and sensory details excerpted from latently gay dreams that had been tormenting the poor hick ever since he'd entered puberty not long before. Teenaged Sammy coerced his cuzzie into driving him to Auntie Louanda's Bordello, which was tucked, like a uterine cyst, in the emptiness of Nevada.

There, especially in the darkest small-town nighttime, a six-foot-six-inch, two-hundred-and-eighty-three-pound fifteen year old had no trouble gaining admittance.

Bryce, the muscular but obviously adolescent chauffeur, had to wait outside in Uncle Rusty's pickup, huddled among dog-eared piles of Mormon choral sheet music, trying to keep his hands off his gorgeous self, and fervently petitioning an especially svelte Lamb of God, magnetized, by the deliberate hand of his mom, to the dash.

"Hey, Fifi. Run fetch muh cuzzie one o' them glossy maggerzines, plus a flashlight. And a big ol' box o' damn Kleenex! Yaw-yaw-yaw!"

Old Sambo modified his accent at such moments without even being aware of it. He was, after all, a congenital and irreversible Utahn, which is to say a terminal chameleon. He had to take Bryce's word for it next morning that he'd sounded like such a perfect ass.

And, tonight on the geothermal formation, Sam regaled the mute intruder, his fellow dry Utahn, with mouth-watering descriptions of the sparkly bottles of real liquor behind the bar—upside-down, for hell's sake!—and the black velvet painting of a nekkid gurl with huge gold bonkers.

And don't forget to mention the actual three-D nekkid gurls—pros-*tit*-toots!—ranged according to size, shape and function in front of the juke box. Surely, God's own tumbling plenty was represented in that line-up, and glory be to Him for dappled things. Each purred or snarled a non-Biblical, ostensibly onomatopoeic moniker that Sammy, with his innate good taste, immediately forgot; so he just held out a finger and grunted.

"Wow! He pointed at the pitcher! How much sh'd we charge him to dork the pitcher?"

And the legit patrons, leathery prole-types slumping in the livid shadows, would reach for concealed lethal things, assuming Sammy was making fun of them when he replied with some Arkansawyer-esque bit of asininity—

"Naw, naw, ladies, you got me all wrong. I don't want ter feck nobody. Just put it in and slide it around a leedle bit, that's all. Yaw-yaw-yaw!"

On the jukebox was somebody whose throat kept going "gunka-gunka" while singing the following:

I caught'cha honky-tonkin' with-a my best friend;
The thing to do was quit'cha
But I should of left then.
Now I'm too old to quit'cha,
But I still get sore
When you come home a-feelin' for the
Knob on the do-o-o-o-o-o-o-o-or.

The madame, a permanent fixture, would sling Sammy complimentary stingers, which he obediently guzzled to cloak his chronic teen halitosis under the creme de menthe. Her night-colored face was so absolutely motionless behind those rhinestoned harlequin spectacles, that Sammy caught his eyes searching for electronic speakers concealed about her vast, shiny person when he heard her say, "How you old Unker Rusty? Ain't seen him in days. You tell him the gals all says hey."

Upon overhearing the tall tale Sammy whined into the gals' ears, i.e., his benzedrine palsy and herpes-horror-induced impotence were chromosomal afflictions, stemming from H-bomb tests in the sterile wastes just outside the back door, why, Auntie Louanda would open up her big black heart, and would neglect a whole Showdeo-rodeo of Brahma bull-humpers in favor of this poor, gangling, ill mutant. She'd nurture Sammy with free Brandies Alexander, gently swirling in extra shots of nutritious Guernsey cream to cushion the hard stuff.

Regardless of what he would tell his cuzzie on the long drive home, old Sambo wound up doing nothing more or less lascivious than talking the night away with his Negroid 'nother-mother; for Auntie Louanda was a bottomless coal mine, bursting with tons of invaluable dirt about The Business and its various manifestations across the increasingly horny nation: pimps are being phased out in the Big Apple, cat houses phased in, owned and operated exclusively by liberated pros-*tit*-toots; men are no longer needed, no bouncers, even—have you ever tried to stand up against a dozen pissed-off working girls?

Heck no thank you, Ma'am! Although we could use a couple of them on this sultry solfatara tonight.

Speaking of pissing off such persons—out in the gravel parking lot, Cuzzie-wuzzie had meanwhile been keeping Fifi bending over the pickup window bare-assed. Like a good classless American boy, Bryce democratically expected her to be, deep down inside, delicate and trembling like himself, another Sonia Marmeladov. So he nervously twiddled the steering wheel between his thigh muscles and tried to engage her in soul talk.

"What, um, insights have you gained into humanity from this, er, job?"

"I'm no diesel dyke, if that's what you mean, queerbait," snarled Fifi, grabbing the fuck-books, the flashlight and the Kleenex and slamming the doors of Paradise in Bryce's maroon face.

* * * *

"My cuzzer and I were, I'd guesstimate, about your age back then, son."

Suddenly, the kid looked up from wrecking his share of the peyote. For the first time all night, through his paralytic grimace, he exhibited more-or-less full powers of speech. Looking every bit as vicious and perverted as Edgar Bergen insinuating things into a wooden doll's oral cavity, he sizzled and hissed, "Yeah, but it was

68

the mid- to late-sixties. Didn't you see God? You never saw God in the mid- to late-sixties? And the early seventies?"

Sam was about to yell, "Nyah-hah, so you can talk!" and nudge him in the floating ribs. But there was something anxious and astonished in his voice that made it seem urgent to deal immediately with his pitiful question.

After all, an oldster dispensing wisdom to a youngster on top of a geothermal formation in the moonlit nighttime really has no business implying that the Golden Age was nothing but a long, smelly visit to a whorehouse, even if such an assertion is fundamentally true. Sam had a responsibility to tell the kid something more.

So he thought hard for about forty seconds, meanwhile keeping an eye on the east for any rosy dawn-fingers that might claw their way over the brink. He furrowed his brow for effect, and caused the piling-up pleats of forehead flesh to push his eyeballs inward and downward a bit. He was being serious now.

And, ever so gradually—as Sam's unhappy neighbor fretted around the base of Golgotha and did those shouting sorts of stage whispers to the effect that Sam should "Run him off! Run him off! It's well-nigh milkin' time!"—the memory-doors creaked open onto a passageway, a luminescent chartreuse tunnel, leading back to the night when Sam did, indeed, get a look at The Beyond.

"Way back when I was a mere callow stripling like yourself, m'boy," said Sam—

* * * *

"On one of those endless rides home from Auntie Louanda's, during the night-portion of a school-day when several classmates and I had dropped some Mr. Natural for the frog-pithing and -vivisection unit of biology class, Brycie-pootums finally got tired of hearing about it instead of doing it (or having it done to him—I don't recall which), and he burst into tears. He stopped Unker Rusty's pickup with an ultimatum (the subliterate

69

rube pronounced in 'ul-tomato'): either he and I climb straight into the back and do what I supposedly just did at Auntie Louanda's, or he, muscular lumpen-peasant that he is, dumps me off, right there in the middle of the midnight desert, to have my poor red-haired noggin scalped and punctured and sucked dry by wild Uncompahgres and picked clean by buzzards before sunrise.

"Well, son, as you may well imagine, it came to blows (no pun intended, necessarily). I remember laughing so hard as to give myself a stitch in my left side, then losing the proverbial 'it.' I briefly came to, flat on my ass on top of a waffled skunk in the middle of the highway, with a turquoise eighteen-wheeler bearing down on me, and quickly learned that the old ethological chestnut about a deer frozen in headlights does not apply to Homo sapiens—

"I land in a mess of oxidized Nephi Creme Soda cans and nettles and salt, all four limbs and twenty digits cold and numb, tingling, no circulation. And then, all at once, the wiseacre razzer, the color announcer to my ball game, my logorrheic consciousness, shuts up. All verbiage is cleared away from a yellow sky, for the length of time it takes to blink once—"

* * * *

"Oh yes!" cried the Killer of Niller. He allowed his ruined brain fruit to slop and dribble through his fingers. "The death experience! That's what hallucinogens were for! To scour out your skull so you could see God! In the sixties! What—" his spinal cord flipped three times in anguished anticipation, like a damp towel in a locker room "—what'd you see?"

At first Sam withheld it, for the kid's sake, because of his earnest face and tender years. Sam protested, in a masculine VFW-type voice, that he didn't want to talk about it.

"That'd be an indiscretion, li'l fella. Like snickering to your buddies about a peek up the skirt of some vast and terrible flirt."

70

The enthusiasm for this discussion, which Sam had been enjoying well enough, abruptly drained from the boy, like ichor from hickeys on birthday sixteen. The snide little "posht" that puffed out of his button nose as much as said, "Oh sure, you doddering coot. 'Indiscretion.' You probably never saw beyond the pucker of your prepuce in the first place. And if you did, you obviously haven't enough psychic energy left over to remember it as anything more than a slight pre-seminal emission. You were feeling all goosey-woosey over the cloddish prospect of servicing this butch cousin of yours whom I keep hearing so much about. Really on your mind, this Brycie, isn't he? After all these decades? Kissing cousin? Hmmm? Old fart. Lecher. Pederast in the past-perfect. Get thee to a proctology clinic."

Sam was not about to settle for the type of reaction that he'd given his own dad's and grampa's and uncles' fond reminiscences for more than a third of a century. So he sat up straight and said, "All right, Sonny Jim. I'll tell you what I saw when I got One with the Goddamn Cosmos in the path of that big rig. Are you ready?"

No response.

"Well, I hope you're ready," huffed Sam, "because I sure am. So, here goes. Okay?"

It was hard to tell if the brazen trespasser was even listening anymore. The time had come to eject him from the premises. This was not a dude ranch around here.

* * * *

"I saw the yellow heavens sundered, and there, in the silence, staring me flat in the face was—" Sam paused, in order to achieve the full emotional impact, then concluded, in round tones, "—Zero! Cipher! Null Set!"

* * * *

"No!" cried the boy, jumping to his feet, kicking up clouds of white dust. "I'm the one that's seen Beyond, not you! I've seen! Lots of times!"

And Junior here began prancing up and down the crater, squishing whole alternative universes of sweet succulent buds under his scale-model combat boots, haranguing Sam with some neo-hip-religio-blab, to the effect that you gotta love persons' minds, and not just what's contained in persons' minds, but you gotta love the very physical substance that comprises persons' minds, and in the act of loving this substance you may pave the way to seeing Beyond. All this was derivative of some twaddle as old as the Carpocratian gnostics, but twisted, comically bent around this twit's Salt Lake City accent, to sound vital, fresh, pertinent.

He pranced way too close to Nature's orifice, affecting each of the stage mannerisms of that other perpetual Utah teenager, Donny Osmond: the same well-coached sexlessness voided from the same squeaky rosebud mouth; the same fretful pettishness glossed over with the same rows of well-flossed toothinesses, peeking from the same, yes, Mormon Smile.

It never unflexes, not even when someone curses their plural parents in their faces: the vitamin D-enriched smile of folks who have Our Heavenly Father by the short-and-curlies, who know the Answer to all the Great Questions. You can't pose them a problem that'll befuddle them.

Sam was faced with the fabled Mormon smile, and it was getting more and more difficult to return his interlocutor's gaze and simultaneously to maintain a settled stomach. The fruits of tonight's harvest were not helping. But Sam continued scarfing them anyway, now that the performance had begun. This was turning out to be a twin rite of mutual self-mortification, a double header.

And then, just as Donny, Jr., started whirling and swishing like a dervish around the vaporish maw, Sam felt a tiny claw grasp his shoulder from behind. He jumped so far and fast in surprise that it felt as though the flap of flesh on the crown of his head had shifted down over his eyebrows forever.

The tiny claw belonged to his neighbor, holder of the deed to this conduit to dissolution. The unhappy man was crouching in terror behind Sam's left love handle. Having apparently lost confidence in Sam's ability to play the bouncer tonight, he had swallowed his own cowardice and bellied up the side of the geothermal formation. Judging from the smell of him, he'd also swallowed a complement of "weasel piss," the Mormon-style three-point-two percent beer, which never had any effect on Sam, but seemed to alter the locals' personalities well enough.

Patting the brownish-orange muzzle of a derelict splatter-gun that he'd dragged up with him, he croaked in a mouse whisper, "Got'cha covered, Big Red. She's loaded with rock salt."

"Un-iodized, no doubt," replied Sam in a voice loud enough to make his neighbor wince and consider scrabbling back down to safety.

"Not so loud!" he pleaded. "Pot-licker'll hear us!"

"Not likely."

Young Master Osmond over there had decided to punctuate his harangue with a few rousing soprano choruses of the Mormon anthem "Come, Come Ye Saints," which is based on the chord changes of Eddy Fisher's "O-o-oh My Papa-a-a." The coyotes sang harmony, and it seemed likely that Nilly-Willy's maw might be awakened any minute by the infernal ruckus.

Even though his deepest convictions had just been offended, the stunted stranger retained that Smile, containing in quintessence everything unregenerate about today's far-western youth. They'd never let this teeny-bopper into Auntie Louanda's Hookshoppe. And if he ever killed anyone's daughter, it was with charm.

Up close, beery and damp, came the whisper into Sam's auditory meatus: "What frosts me is the pot-licker did less time in the damn pokey for doin 'trocious thangs to our pore li'l gal than he did for bein' sack-religious on his damn proselytizin' mission back east."

"Proselytizing mission?" cried Sam.

"Would you keep it down? This ain't choir practice in the ding-dang tabernapple. That's jest what I said: mission. He's a returned mish, dishonor'bly dish-charged. They say he done 'trocious thangs 'n stuff to his damn missionary companion. Somethin' nutty like boiled him 'n shackled him 'n drove him bonkers. I am here to tellya, Big Red, when our good Latter-Day-Saint boys fall off their palomino, they don't mess 'round, y'know?"

"Mission?" Sam repeated with growing incredulity. "How old's this crazy guy?"

"Damn sight older'n you."

"But I thought—"

"Us too, at first. Thang is, these crazy fuckers—'xcuse m' French—they don't age fast. It's like they ain't got a damn conscience gnawing away, drivin 'em to drink and self-aboose like the rest of us."

"Come, come ye sai-i-i-ints, no toil nor labor fe-e-e-ear!" shrieked the boy—rather, man. Or maybe guy. And, as he shrieked, it remained even still: the vomity rictus of Donny Osmond, Merlin Olsen and Orrin Hatch. How can their names start with an "O" when their lips remain stretched wide to make an "E"? Smile and smile and be a villain.

Sam's neighbor was huddled and snuggled way too close, like a grooming rhesus monkey. He had jockeyed his buck teeth and chappy lips only millimeters from Sam's ear-hole, presumably to aid whispered communication over the ruckus. He propped his splatter-gun's crumbling muzzle against Sam's bare shoulder.

Oblivious of his audience's doubling, the ageless creature continued writhing before them. He squatted down, gathered up another chunk of calcium carbonate, and started whacking it against his own forehead to emphasize some of his finer eschatological points. Blood trickled down to gild his tetanal smile and trace the crevices between his big wholesome incisors and canines. Like many divinely inspired homilists, he was giving himself up to the Paraclete, and losing awareness of his audience, assuming the

74

Pentecostal tongue-flame that rose from the hole newly bashed in his head would light the way through his subordinate clauses, like the pillar of fire leading the usual folks through the usual wilderness.

"This li'l turd-snapper spended most of his 'dult life in the damn nut-house, anyways, so's he ain't had wimmen 'n bills drivin' him to his early grave neither. Our taxes, yours 'n mine, Big Red, been footin' that little cake-soaker's bill all these years, through the damn sexy-sixties, feedin' him that hot kwee-zeen they serve down to State Mental Horspiddle. So he's stayed all smooth and shiny and purdy and smiley, like one o' them toy dolls they always show bitin' pore little gals in the damn scary movies. Red lips 'n all."

Sam's neighbor patted his relic splatter-gun and released a three-point-two percent belch, redolent with chemicals and confidence.

"Sum-bitch'd better not be pullin' no more scary movie crapola round here. Leastways not real soon. Or they'll be hell t' pay. He's got you 'n me to corn-tend with. Right, Big Red One?"

"Um, well—"

Meanwhile Nilla-Killa, too, had shifted to a more emphatic rhetorical stance. Down on hands and knees, he had reassumed the peyote-plucking position, and now heaved his reflections straight down into the vagina dentata. Sam considered reaching out a long leg and sending him to apologize to Nilla. But that wouldn't be running him off, exactly. Quite the opposite, in fact.

"Jumpin' Jesus!" cried Sam's neighbor in a stage-whisper, "Don't let 'im get so close to th' edge o' that raunchy toilet!"

"What, you're worried about his safety?"

"Not his safety. Ours! For hell's sakes, talkin' at the great white telephone is what set him off in the first place."

"Set him off? In what sense of the—"

"Near's ol' Deptysherf could re-*con*-struct, him 'n silly Nillie was up here courtin', an' she came on a bit too hellacious, as wimmen in that branch of our genealogy are prone t' do. So, of course, he started havin' tummy problems 'n excused hisself, as good L.D.S. boys are instructed to do by their neighborhood bishops. And he seen somebody or some goddamn thang down there inside my fumarole or solfatara, or whatever. And the sum-bitchin' kid jest went bonkers is all. Started chuckin' boulders 'n hollerin' bout monsters from the finny deeps, Leviathan and so forth, then took off a-runnin' through the damn scrub oak. Took half a barb wire fence with him. He come back when everbody but you-know-who was asleep in Dream Land."

At the mention of that unfocused continent, the poor victim's plural papa seemed to go into neutral. He sighed, and shifted to a more comfortable attitude of prostration behind Sam's goose-bumped hugeness. Idly clinking a few gnawed fingernails against his firearm, he settled in to watch the monster show. An inordinate amount of time passed.

"Oh, for fuck's sake!" cried Sam.

"Beg-pard?"

"Are you going to tell me?"

"Tell you what?"

"Wha—what'd he do to her?" Sam whispered, knowing the answer, deep in his guts, as they say. But not nearly deep enough. Already halfway up the esophagus.

"Somethin' nuttier'n a damn hoot-owl's what he done," began Nilly-Willy's quasi-stepdad, warming to the tale. "It seems that—"

Some episodes of queasiness manifest themselves with such conviction that, when we finally are able to separate our cold-sweat-glued eyelids, we expect to see, distributed across the vast expanse of our bare body, great throbbing gouts of our own scarlet entrails, which will flop off the ill-defined edges of our torso and soak into our poor inadequate jockey briefs.

Sam's neighbor didn't seem to notice any eruptions. He was holding forth now, building his own momentum for once, like a man. Splatter-gun tucked close at hand, he'd gotten up off his belly, and was now on his knees, the better to bear down verbally on the hole in the side of Sam's head, as if it belonged to the sweet prince's father.

"Now our dang neighborhood bishops're always preachin' at us 'bout yer blast-phemy 'gainst yer Holy Ghost bein' yer One Unpardonable Sin, y'know? Well, sir, right 'bout now I'm thinkin' the ol' Prophet/ Seer/ Revelator up there in Salt Lake oughta *de*-cree that the Second Unpardonable Sin is when you're gittin' a hold o' somebody's li'l nineteen-year-old princess and—"

"Boo-wharr-ghhhk-mmf-bah!" said Sam's upper gastro-intestinal tract, independent of his will. And again: "Mmm-blaght-urp-ghhhk."

He raised his forehead from a semi-solid puddle in his lap, and saw reflected a lumpy clown face. Pert red tennis-ball nose, fuzzy arched eyebrows, shiny yellow mouth wearing, ooooh, such a festive grin! Smeared on with indelible grease paint! He had pranced the nocturnal fumarole with such quaint anecdotes!

"—ain't that one heck of a note? Talk about brain-fuck. Talk about givin' head. Boy, that'd cure me o' sex forev—whatsa matter, Big Red? You're lookin' awful dang chipper, considerin' the tale o' woe I been tellin'. Smug as a hog in slop, I'd say. Where's yer compassion at? Where's yer feller feelin'? Maybe you sh'd consider wipin' that guffaw off'n yer mug afore Nilloid's maw starts clankin' them milk buckets around."

It sounded like a fair warning, and was accompanied by a shudder on the word "maw."

In fact, now that he mentioned it, Sam did feel a lot better, thank you very much. Marvelously better. The Hour of Lead had passed, and the Great Noonday approached. Sam was unbending now, a good green Uncompahgre vegetable king. Take, eat, this is my chlorophyll. Do this in remembrance of me.

"You saw Nothing because you never saw anything!" cried the intruder, and focused on Sam. "Degenerate heathen eyes such as yours can never—oh, that's disgusting!"

"Eat me raw."

"But I thought you said you never did that."

77

Sam laughed right in his kisser, gave him another display of puked eucharist, and laughed again through mustache-strained chunks. In sublime hiatal discomfort, he bubbled and splashed amplitudes of full-pulp pepsin.

Showing fastidiousness worthy of a true gourmet, the little cannibal recoiled. He skidded all the way down Golgotha, into the brimming dawn light, and disappeared behind an authentically rustic outbuilding.

"Where you going, Donny?" hooted Sam, whisking him away like a fly with a fistful of strychnine fibers.

Several surprised moo's accompanied the plasma-carbonating shriek of a woman's voice—belonging to Niller's maw, no doubt—followed by the sounds of bare-knuckled mayhem, climaxed by the sight of poor Nilla-Killa bleeding and limping and skedaddling faster'n a partly-squished jackrabbit, taking half a barb wire fence with him, clear across the Salt Flats till the curvature of the planet gobbled him down. The early bird caught the worm after all.

"Pot-licker got lucky this time," said her husband. "Last time he was jest barely able to crawl away. She hates havin' to wail on people. Takes a lot out of the poor ol' gal."

And then some somber, accusing eyes focused on Sam.

He sat up straight and tried to wipe himself off a bit. Assuming the expected facial expression, he said, "What? I ran him off, didn't I?"

Dead Time at the Hospice

I saw comparatively little of Japan.
I did not understand the people at all...
—Aleister Crowley, *Autohagiography*

Cynthia seems to have come barging out of her mom's womb with a gargantuan knack for getting into trouble. That's the only explanation for her life. But when she showed up in Tokyo last month, she outdid herself. Cynthia fucked up so badly, and so creatively, that even the cops were stunned.

The Procurator actually started to weep. He was going to have to rack his brains to fabricate some sort of charge that could be preferred against her. It could take weeks to invent a legalism for such strange and utter badness as our Cynthia's. Meanwhile, he and his fellow muckety-mucks of the law enforcement establishment must grope about for an excuse, and a means, to *disappear* her, in the transitive Argentinean sense.

"She needs to be stashed somewhere," whimpered the Procurator. "The American State Department might take notice any moment and try to pry this pallid succubus from our grasp!"

Cynthia tried not to guffaw too loudly when she heard that last bit. As if the current Unitary Executive could be bothered to interrupt its own *disappearings* of American citizens to rescue her sweet, unsocializable succubus ass.

No less a personage than the Chief of the semi-secret Imperial Police stepped in, on a consultancy basis no doubt. Toddling down from the Togu Palace, he packed no interesting weapons, and came equipped only with a tiny communication device tucked in his boy-sized ear that squeaked and made him twitch rhythmically. But he got to wear special insignia and much cuter shoulder braids than those of his counterparts, the plain old municipal flatfeet.

This Imperial Police dork was the one to come up with the bright idea. Like all peacocks he was intimate with mud, and he knew a puddle just viscous enough for a Cynthia-sized stone to be rolled in without causing too many ripples.

There's a quadrant of Tokyo so obscure that it might as well be stuffed among the acid-rain ravaged bamboos on Okinawa. A relic of civil engineering, this feudal neighborhood's streets proved too anfractuous for our bombs way back in '45. Its labyrinthine alleys baffled our vindictiveness, and remain to this day unrectified and unbaptized in Yankee flames. Search hard as you might for a landmark, you will blunder past no Disney boutique, no Starbucks, no DVD rental shop, no titty bar with curly-headed touts hovering in puddles of jar head barf out front. There's not a single sputtering tubeful of neon in this time-encapsulization of pre-MacArthur Nippon. Such a vacuum-zone is hardly considered Tokyo at all by the sort of people who matter. Nobody youthful nor even youngish thinks of making this scene. Neither the trendy nor the transgressive swing by. Inch-thick eyeshadow, brown lipstick and spiked fake red hair are in as short supply as non-Yakuza tattoos.

Just how unfashionable is this Ookie-Gookie Ward (or whatever the fuck it's called)? Well, it boasts not so much as a single example of those *de rigeur* nightclubs where salary-men piss and shit into diapers while youngish Filipina darvon addicts in nurse outfits go to work with the elbow grease and the lanolin Tidy-Wipes (usually nodding off halfway through the chore). Not a proper Japanese cultural center at all, this Ookie-Gookie Ward. It goes without saying that someone like Cynthia had never heard of the place.

What darker nook in which to conceal shame? What deeper cranny in which to bury a criminoid monstress like Cynthia?

And where better to preserve Japan's pretense that its people are less prone than Africans or gay Americans to contract a certain illness—rather, a whole syndrome of them? In other words,

80

Ookie-Gookie Ward is where Tokyo hides its myriads of AIDS infectees.

So the cops hustled our Cynthia down into an iodine-reeking nook of Metropolitan Police Headquarters, a blind sac in the bowels of the complex, and set about persuading her to submit to a blood test. She let her lack of enthusiasm for such an invasive procedure be known. During the negotiations a standard-issue police truncheon seems to have been produced, and to have removed two-thirds of the suspect's facial epidermis.

"Oka-a-a-ay," she moaned and sizzled through a mouthful of hemorrhage and raggedy tissue. "Now we're getting somewhere."

It just seemed like the natural thing to say at the moment, accompanied by as much of a T. E. Lawrence-style bump and grind as possible under the straitened circumstances. But it shocked and appalled the men present. Masters of the bloodless confession, Nipponese narks rarely need resort to physical contact with yellow male suspects, much less archetypally sacrosanct white women.

Even as her precious bodily fluids were spilt, her peaches-and-cream flesh reamed out, the girl-*gaijin* was calling the shots. On a whim, just for mischief's sake, she overwhelmed her oppressors with the force and malleability of contemporary American sexuality, and all sorts of individuated occidental stuff like that. Cynthia was as far beyond the ken of Douglas MacArthur's "race of twelve year olds" as a clod of photosynthetic Martian soil.

Flustered cop testosterone can always be relied upon to bring down a further application of the old truncheon. This one came across the upper thighs; and Cynthia almost blushed to feel herself creaming her jeans.

"She's a fox-demoness, Boss!" gasped a rickshaw-boy-in-blue. The Procurator and the Grand Inquisitor, as well as the Imperial Police Peacock, all had to concur.

By the most surprising coincidence, her blood test came back positive. This wasn't exactly the Mom-and-Pop corner clinic around here, and it was true that Cynthia was getting the gold card treatment; but still, wasn't the human immunodeficiency virus supposed to take a skosh longer than two minutes to sprout its garish tubers through the old agar-agar? Might the cops have trumped her test results up? Or had Cynthia unwittingly done something in the past one-to-twenty years to embark herself on a headlong course toward slow diapered death? Who cares? She'd learned long ago that life was a crap shoot, heavy on the crap.

Her now-lethal breath was filtered through a surgical mask. The poison-oozing truncheon hole in her face was rendered forever non-threatening by the liberal application of some airplane glue-like spray-on sealant, and covered over with tough plastic sheeting that was held in place by fiberglass strapping, then swathed with a cosmetic layer of traditional cotton batting and white adhesive tape, increasing the circumference of the lady's head by at least fifty percent.

As they carted her off to the bleak nowheresville of Ookie-Gookie Ward, manacled wrist and ankle, Cynthia delivered a laughter-blasted apocalypse, letting it rebound off the cinder brick and linoleum of this fascist fortress—

"The postmodern plague is about to explode on this whore-mongering archipelago! And your craven superstition will only make it worse! Shinto shrines will have waiting lines two miles long! People will die hunkering on queues to bribe one of your twenty thousand gods for deliverance! Entire granite buddhas and jizos will be eroded to dust under the purple-splotched fingers of the diseased devout! My grandpa's fire-bombs will look like a backyard weenie roast by comparison!"

* * * *

Duly bound and hooded, not to mention gagged (much to the relief of everyone else involved), Cynthia was driven by means of an unmarked black-curtained van down roads that resembled fistfuls of flung ramen. America's pugnaciousness finally exploded its way into Ookie-Gookie Land. They stuck her in a crypto-clinic—or maybe hospice described it better.

Her new home was discreetly camouflaged inside an abandoned kindergarten, complete with cast-iron jungle gyms in the yard. Seesaws and tricky bars were coated with various layers of pastel enamel that sloughed off in lead-rich chips, a different shade for each receding year of the place's viability, till bare WWII-vintage metal showed through and made the whole assemblage look like modernist sculpture, tortured and orangish-brown among the rioting weeds. This playground equipment had been idled by the catastrophic graying of Japanese society: most likely the whole block boasted nary a wife that hadn't been mail-ordered from the Philippines, and precious few of them.

On the inside, the kiddy classrooms had been stripped of every vestige of their former color. It was a dreary national health plan-type dump, crawling with crematorium fodder and their unextended families. Centenarian grannies, shame-reamed and internally exiled, fetched messes of attenuated rice gruel for sarcomatous proto-corpses with whom Cynthia was expected to share fraying and fragrant tatami mats.

Soon she was stretched out voluptuously on a makeshift trestle-and-bamboo examination table. With touching gingerliness, and no trace of fear, a lovely gaggle of junior nurses group-chipped the elaborate prophylaxis from her face. Politely (and ever so quietly, so as not to disturb the prostate-packing physicians who spent their lives napping in neighboring classrooms), the nurses inquired as to the how and when of exposure. Having expected a full blown AIDS lesion, they were surprised to see how quickly it was already healing.

"A substratum of proudflesh and granulation tissue is already in place!" one of them marveled in a baby whisper, while the rest closed in to palpate not only the wound, but other even more strapping patches of Cynthia's golden flesh. She showed these slim creatures her breasts.

"God knows there is nothing amiss with your immune system!" they said, with marvel in their exquisite eyes and voices. (Japanese medical types are trained to employ elevated diction while on duty, as it inspires confidence in the hearts of the Confucian doomed.)

"Why did the men put you here, being asymptomatic?" they cried, their sense of justice visibly piqued.

She and her gurney soon constituted the main float in a parade down the corridor. The nurses were eager to show Cynthia around and let her know that the clinic under-staffers, at least, were foursquare behind her—as opposed to the very mature doctors who didn't give a fuck, barely knew she existed, as they snored in mainlined-Dilaudid stupors on patients' usurped futons, or flexed dwarf muscles on the putting green that had been improvised in the playground's abandoned sand box, where the nurses had once meekly suggested a small but therapeutical veggie garden might be grown.

These were among the least brilliant medicos in the country. Too incompetent to practice among regular non-outcast Nihonjin, they were deemed fit only to treat patients sleazy enough to be caught dead with this shameful sickness. They were the medical equivalent of Roman Catholic convent chaplains, who aren't allowed parishes due to a certain characteristic personality defect, and are entrusted with the cure of no souls other than overripe nuns', among whom their otherwise uncontrollable homosexual pederastic urges can be held in check for lack of an object.

It turned out that Tokyo nurses, especially ones of this particular specialty, in addition to being sleek as lynxes swimming in the summertime, were among the few feminized creatures on these islands. They'd undergone consciousness-raising-by-ordeal. One by one, in a most orderly and euphemistic Yamato fashion, they stepped forward and told Cynthia things. Each woman contributed duly to the collective utterance of subdued rage in a piping lisp and whisper like a dreaming baby's, just audible over the moans and farts and shrieks of AIDSies meeting their maker.

"Perhaps Cynthia-san is now looking at the AIDS explosion which will never hit this nation, according to the distinguished spokesman for the Japanese Center for Disease Control."

"Some honorable overseas observers have suggested that HIV might be reported about as often in this country as a certain disservice to women."

"You mean rape?" asked Cynthia.

"Mmm... it could seem so."

"It seems not altogether unlikely, Cynthia-san, that AIDS might still be considered a disease of only our foreign friends; so the natives who catch it are gently persuaded to come to hidden places like this one, where their difficulties will not pose an inconvenience to others less sorely afflicted."

"In this clinic, we are privileged to deliver babies in almost pre-industrial style, for not so many of the doctors, in their wisdom, deem it advisable to lend us their expert assistance. Nor have they seen fit to exercise their well-earned prerogative to allow us the use of the facilities, such as they are. It's not entirely beyond the realm of possibility, Cynthia-san, that they consider the blood and placenta of these unlucky high school girls to be a lethal poison capable of soaking through any number of protective membranes, like some nerve agent discreetly developed by their distinguished moral counterparts in the Self-Defense Forces."

"Perhaps these children's babies could have a very slight chance to be born healthy by avoidance of the birth canal, but we mere humble nurses are far from wise enough to have received training in C-section techniques; and in any case we would find it very difficult to generate the funds needed to adhere to the regulations that pertain to surgical treatment of AIDS victims."

"Yes, it has been suggested by the National Agency for Epidemiological Studies that it might not be an altogether bad idea for health care workers to employ triple gloves, burnable bedding and gowns, disposable syringes, goggles and scalpels, and so on. If a nurse wants to make a note of her patient's progress, she is gently requested to throw away the pen, but first to autoclave it for seven hours."

"Insane! Alarmist! Hypercautionary!" shrieked Cynthia, settling into her role as the barbarian who didn't know better than to insert plainspoken extrapolations on these exquisitely controlled cries of anguish. "So these poor teenybopper punklets," she hollered, "themselves under an early death sentence, are forced to infect their own babies, right? And the cocksucking leeches' attitude is, 'Who gives a shit? Certain people shouldn't be allowed to procreate.' Am I right, or what? Huh? What do you think, girlfriends?"

"We have heard what Cynthia-san is saying. When such difficult questions arise, the most venerable physicians can always fall back on their grandmothers' Buddhist doctrine—"

"These old lechers?" scoffed Cynthia at top volume. "I'm an expert myself in certain fields of human endeavor, and I can tell you, just by looking at the green bags under their eyes, that when the sun goes down they're as impious as any in Japan."

"*So, desuka?* According to their grandmothers' faith, the tiny souls that exit the earth several times each day by way of this clinic can always try again in a reincarnated body."

"So it's okay," blurted Cynthia, "even theologically laudable, to condemn them to death."

"One might be inclined to think thoughts to that effect."

These nurses had been informed of their new patient's unnameable act. But, far from jaundicing their view of her, it put them in solidarity with Cynthia, and made them want to sneak around and help her however they could; for, soft-spoken as they were, they hated the whole paternalistic scheme of Japanese things that had caused so many of their sisters to be confined here to languish and die in third-world conditions, while the sex-touring, whore-mongering salary-men who'd infected them were allowed to go free—

"That is, until the purple sarcomas and the uncontrollable diarrhea set in, and the men begin to lose face by going out."

"Yes, then the most worthy gentlemen are forced to stay home and order up Tidy Wipe house calls from our Filipina sisters, while, perhaps, their wives look the other way."

"And still they might possibly find it very difficult to persuade themselves to wear condoms."

As she toured the hush-hush hospice and listened to the nurses, Cynthia felt a strong sense of comfort—so far. Moral indignation was her element, especially when aimed at well-deserving old men. She even forgot that she was supposed to be a prisoner, in her delight and surprise at discovering a whole secret coven of like-minded females, the first she'd encountered on this rim of the big rim-job called the Pacific.

But then they did something which made her feel that the truncheon-wielding cops had sent her to exactly the right place if they wanted to torture her, to flay the emotional skin off her psychic bones. The nurses recruited her to help comfort one of the doomed little ones. Cynthia begged to be let off the hook, but they wouldn't take no for an answer.

"We're understaffed," they said, looking the other way and going about their business, leaving an enormously tiny burden in her arms. "This little girl likes the sunshine."

Cynthia sat in the Tokyo smog, rocking a stranger on a jungle gym that was crumbling and rotting away almost as fast as the youngsters who'd never play on it. At first she couldn't look at the creature cradled in her elbow, but just noticed the diaper smell. So far so good: the best way to convince yourself they're not worth the bother is to sniff them.

But she noticed it wasn't the regular smell. It was like nothing so much as turpentine: a pungent, yet not altogether unpleasant odor, as if this kid, in being removed so soon from the temptations of manifested existence, hadn't developed whatever it is in most babies' bowels that already inspires repugnance in all but the most devoted mom. Cynthia was whiffing prelapsarian poo-poo, before the apple slid down the gullet and started the process of corruption.

The little girl wanted to play. But she was too weak to lift her arms. So, through a habitual haze of pain, she contented herself with making naughty faces, as if to say, "Teach me how to raise hell, girlfriend. I was born with the knack."

Cynthia made a few faces back, though not the ones she intended. The troublesome American seemed to have picked up some sort of secondary virus. She was experiencing a watery discharge, colorless and copious, from the eyes. Respiration was irregular.

The Home of the Brave

*The real foundations of contemporary Japanese life are the
achievements of the Aryan peoples.*
—Mein Kampf

A cement mixer roars across a riverside construction site in
the blackest depths of the Hiroshima night. Ishida-san, a noted figure in the local power structure, has chosen this location for his
new pachinko parlor, which he intends to be the most stupendous
gambling hall west of Osaka. Under hissing arc-lights, work is being done around the clock, to realize his dream quickly.

A huge billboard out front reads, in both Japanese and English—

THE HOME OF THE BRAVE
GRAND OPENING SOON

The old man himself stands right in the middle of things,
overseeing the work, a cigar pursed unlit between his lips.

A fabulous array of neon lights, all colors and configura-
tions, has been wired into the fresh facade. And, on the top, where
the steeple might be if this structure were consecrated to a god
other than Mammon, a gigantic fiberglass Statue of Liberty has
been installed. She is very buxom, with moon-sized turquoise eyes
and lemon-yellow hair that curls and tumbles richly from under her
spiked crown.

The ultimate finishing touch is being lowered from the
polluted heavens by a yellow crane. It's an almost full-sized epoxy-resin King Kong. The destination of this whale-sized monkey
seems, for all the world, to be the shapely shoulders of Lady Liberty.

* * * *

As furtively as possible, a little archaeology professor from Hiroshima Municipal Women's College scales the clanking chain link fence that defines this construction site. He starts to poke around in the shadows.

This professor is a native of the city. But he wears a beard and dresses in rumpled pseudo-proletarian clothes, adhering very self-consciously to the western academic style. His efforts to look like a foreigner have caused many of his more conservative countrymen to question his patriotism.

But he is not here tonight on a political mission. He believes this stretch of riverbank to be of great archaeological significance. Assuming that his research and calculations are correct, this is the former location of the harem of Daimyo Mohri, Hiroshima's founder, and the very author of the local way of life. If the professor's not mistaken, the soil under Mr. Ishida's new gambling den could bristle with priceless 400-year-old relics that prove Mohri was not Japanese at all, but a transplanted ethnic Korean.

Merely to whisper such heresy would be to enrage the extreme rightist community, of which Ishida-san is not exactly a member. But he shares several friendly connections with the fanatical super-patriots, and has been known to do certain of their more unpleasant chores for them. He also dabbles in Filipina sex slavery, methamphetamine distribution and labor racketeering.

The archaeology professor does not worry about these ominous connections, for he cares only about The Truth. And he is convinced that Ishida-san is burying this town's cultural heritage under slabs of reinforced concrete. So, tonight, he pries back a couple such slabs, turns over a few shovelfuls of mud—and does, indeed, discover an artifact from the time of the great Daimyo Mohri.

The professional pleasure in his face turns to adolescent glee, then intensifies into megalomania. He must think he's been suddenly rendered immortal, for he chooses this moment to deliver the muddy item, personally, to Ishida-san, along with an ultimatum.

No longer caring if he is seen trespassing, the unprepossessing professor pockets his find and treks out across the construction area, toward a large house trailer, which serves as a twenty-four-hour on-site administrative office. On its front awning is hung the sinister-looking *kanji* emblem of Ishida-san's underworld organization, big and conspicuous in the artificial light.

* * * *

Unlike most such temporary offices, it's lavishly appointed inside, complete with black-velvet paintings of tigers, a wet bar, and even a fake European-style fireplace with a deep mantelpiece for Ishida-san's gentlemanly bric-a-brac. The old mobster has decided to pitch camp here, so he can personally supervise things until the work is done.

The unlit cigar still clenched between his lips, he sits behind a grand mahogany desk, shuffles invoices, and tries not to eavesdrop on a conversation that's being conducted outside. His number-one lieutenant, a sallow, reptilian fellow, is standing sentry at the stoop and speaking to a couple of problematical-looking persons.

"This project is the pride and joy of our *oyabun*'s work life, just as his daughters are the jewels of his love life. The old man beheld this place in an actual mystic vision..."

The lieutenant is addressing a couple of teen bikers, known in Japan as *bosozoku*. They wear purple and green spike hairdos, brown lipstick, and buttock-exposing cutaway leather jeans. On the backs of their jackets is emblazoned the name of their gang:

THE KELOID KROWD

In the whole universe, these two "bozos" want nothing more than to be admitted to the ranks of the Japanese Mafia. To that end, they've been hanging around Ishida-san's trailer for weeks, sleeping in the mud and peeing in the weeds, just so they can be available to fetch him canned coffee and rice balls, or even their own sisters, if he so requires.

Through an emotion-constricted voice box, the lieutenant is saying, "It's his dream. Let me tell you just how dear this project is to his old heart. Our *oyabun*'s not the type of person who gets rushed very easily, but—"

"No shit," blurts the less intelligent biker.

The lieutenant nails this callow boy to the still-warm asphalt with a serrated glance, which says, "It would be better for your health never to interrupt me again." Then he preens himself a tad and continues where he left off.

He explains that Ishida-san has given orders to toss this parlor up in record time. And today The Home of the Brave stands on absolutely no foundation at all, in violation of every building code ever enacted on this earthquake-prone archipelago. The law has no relevance in the life of such a mighty man.

The *bosozoku* suck in the lieutenant's every word like babes at the pap. And he, in turn, has taken a paternal interest in these youthful hangers-on. He likes to feel them looking up to him. So, when the archaeology professor comes striding out of the night like some hairy-faced ghost, the lieutenant tries hard to conceal his momentary terror.

The intruder heads straight for Ishida-san's door, neither bothering to explain his unauthorized presence on the premises, nor troubling himself to ask permission of the sentry—who is no longer frightened, but extremely angry. Not about to lose face in front of representatives of the Keloid Krowd, the lieutenant promptly knocks the professor flat on his back and removes the contents of his pockets, including the ancient object. This he passes through the window to Ishida-san, who has risen from his desk and pulled back the lacy curtains in mild curiosity.

The left side of his head is being ground into the mud by a *bosozoku*'s hobnailed boot, so the shaggy academic must shout to be heard. "Ishida-san! Bribe me generously, or I go public with that item and all work ceases around here!"

There's a third alternative, which doesn't occur to him until the old man nods his head gently, and the razor-sharp blade of an exquisitely-crafted Samurai-style *wakizashi* blade glints in the arc light.

"See now," the lieutenant primly says, taking this opportunity to provide his two admirers with some practical instruction, "you don't just jab straight on like this. His sternum gets in the way."

When the tip of the knife clicks against his breast bone, the archaeologist looks more surprised than pained.

As the lecture-demonstration in basic Yakuza skills continues, the old man retires from the window and settles himself in a sumptuous green leather armchair, imported from the Occident and sized accordingly. He looks like a little boy usurping Daddy's favorite perch, as he examines the potsherd. It's intricately decorated in the ancient Korean style.

"This is the proper angle," says the voice outside, "between these two ribs. Slice in, firmly, to get through the muscle fibers, and then up, up, up. Come on, don't be so polite about it. I mean really up! Try again... Okay, now watch his eyes. Count to ten... See that? The life goes out at a leisurely pace, and he sort of snuggles into himself with a sigh, like a tired baby at bedtime. That's because we have just cleanly sliced his left ventricle in two, in the efficient and effective manner of our proud Samurai ancestors."

Ishida-san stands, traverses his office, and arranges his new curio attractively on the ersatz mantelpiece. He squints his eyes and tilts his head, to check the effect in this particular slant of light.

"Now, if the old man told us to keep this person alive, for whatever reason, and we didn't want him to run away, we'd do this to the soles of his feet... It's a technique we learned from La Cosa Nostra, except we improved on it. If you slash only in one direction like the Italians do, sometimes a tough man can bear the pain and use his feet anyway. So we make the mark of the Chinese cha-

character *sei*... But you boys are probably junior high dropouts, so you can't be expected to know your *kanji*, right? Well, let's just say it looks like a tic-tac-toe game. And it makes a wound in the pads of his feet that never heals up, not even if he lives another six or seven weeks."

"With his eyes bugged out, and that beard," observes one of the youngsters, "he looks just like an American."

"Hey, numb-nuts," snarls the lieutenant, "down here. We're working on the other end of him, in case you haven't noticed." Then, in a gentler, more patronizing tone: "It's best not to look at their eyes after you've tucked them in. Their soul is looking for a place to hide from the devil, and it might just choose your body." He pauses for that sobering admonition to sink in. "And now, you ignorant boys, I want you to think hard. Under these circumstances, do I even need to ask how we dispose of our handiwork?"

Ishida-san hears this last question and breaks into a small, fond smile. He gazes out the window, across the site of his future dream palace, and his eyes alight upon the cement mixer, whose roaring continues unabated.

By this time, King Kong has successfully mounted the Statue of Liberty, and is being fastened on with sturdy rivets. For now, until the next seismic event rumbles along, the big plastic monkey perches right where Ishida-san wants him to perch. With the rough-edged wit that appeals so strongly to the Japanese working class, he dry-humps Lady Liberty's left eye socket.

* * * *

Later that night, on a moonlit stretch of riverbank further out of town, a pair of thugs, one recognizable as Ishida-san's favorite lieutenant, are pulling someone with a beard from the back of a beautiful Toyota van. The little archaeologist looks, for all the world, every bit as dead as the flotilla of carp carcasses through which the two gangsters must tiptoe on their way to dump him in the water.

94

The earth begins to move, in a moderately strong example of the temblors that rock western Japan a couple times each year. It's nothing unusual; but, under these special circumstances, it's enough to fill any self-respecting Yakuza with superstitious dread. Their palms get so sweaty that they accidentally drop the rumpled corpse in the toxic Ohtagawa mud, cracking his poorly-cast cement overshoes on a culvert. Two dead, bare feet appear in the moonlight, the flesh pulled away from the Chinese characters which the lieutenant earlier slashed into their soles.

Obviously, this is an ill omen. So they abandon the archaeologist on the bank, leaving this disposal job half done, and run to cower and cringe in their vehicle.

Whimpering among blood puddles on the plush-carpeted floor, the lieutenant rubs and puffs and licks his Shinto fetishes, and tries to bribe his countless gods for deliverance, while the handsome vehicle bounces and squeaks on its shocks, and the temblor continues.

* * * *

At this moment, more unhappy things are happening in Bosozokuland, which is located further downstream, under the turnpike bridges, where barge locks flush the dregs of Japan's inland sea uphill in a crumby backwash. In the Keloid Krowd's hangout, teen bikers in outlandish punk-derivative garb are working on their motorcycles and hot rods, by the light of a vast styrofoam bonfire that fills this whole quadrant of the north Pacific with a black syrupy smoke of pure dioxin.

The bozos are copulating, sparring, shooting up, and covering every surface with incredibly beautiful graffiti. Skulls, mushroom clouds, vaginas and English words are spray-painted everywhere with effortless, hallucinatory, *Ukiyoe*-like clarity. Nylon paint-inhaling bags flutter in the air like giant dandelion flocculi, and the surface of the water is only visible when a garbage barge's wake jostles its glistening skin of spent prophylactics.

The Keloid Krowd clubhouse is less a proper building than a lean-to, composed of discarded tatami mats. But the walls possess just enough integrity to shield the eyes of any but the most morbidly curious onlooker from the goings-on within.

The number-one lieutenant's two apt pupils are practicing the assassination techniques they learned at The Home of the Brave construction site. For a fine Samurai knife and an archaeology professor they have substituted an aluminum rat-tail comb and an aged, incontinent wino. So far, they've only succeeded in injuring him.

When they feel the earth shed some of its solidity, they abandon their practice, adjust their green and purple coifs, and sprint outside, where they join dozens of comrades in manning the throttles of various souped-up rice burners. This is a regular Keloid Krowd drill.

The bikers rev in unison, trying to frighten the disruptive subterranean spirits off with a blast of infernal racket from their unmuffled engines. They almost sound like an inbred Appalachian prayer-house choir belting out a chorus or two of "Amazing Grace."

* * * *

Meanwhile, at the Home of the Brave, the Goddess of Democracy and her tall, dark lover are having their first scrape. The freshly installed King Kong begins to slip from his moorings. His epoxy-resin thighs groan, creak and crack against Lady Liberty's cheeks and earlobes. Ishida-san's contribution to Hiroshima's renovated skyline is far from secure.

The spectacular gambling hall is shifting on its non-foundation. The focus of King Kong's affection is no longer Lady Liberty's left eye socket, but has slipped down several yards, to a lower aperture. Now he's being fellated by the mammoth dream queen.

In succumbing to gravity, the monkey's lower mandible has caught on one of the spikes of her fiberglass crown, like a rainbow trout on a hook, and his mighty neck has snapped backward. He adores the gouts of sulfur and diesel that broil overhead, and bares his Volkswagen-sized canines in ecstasy.

I Was a Teenage Rent-a-Frankenstein

...it became a thing such as even Dante could not have conceived...
—Mary Wollstonecraft Shelley

Years ago, fresh-faced and pretty much normal, my favorite cousin, Pynn Barkdull, went on a Mormon mission to Salem, Massachusetts. After serving out the appointed two years, he came back on the Greyhound appearing every bit as wholesome as when he'd left, admirably concealing the fact that he could see and feel fiery blisters erupting from his flesh, and could hear, inside his own skull, the tormented screeches of every witch that had ever been hanged or pressed in that town.

Once ensconced in his parents' house trailer, way out in the middle of the Salt Flats, Pynn took to his bed, and begged to be administered the secret Mormon laying-on-of-hands ceremony. Refused this drastic measure on the grounds that he was "just a tad tuckered out, an' re-quired nothin more 'n a few days snoozin in the ol' fart sack," Pynn took matters into his own mysteriously white-gloved hands.

With a histrionic gesture of his long arm, he scooped the big blue jar of Noxema cold cream and the decorator box of facial-quality tissue off his night stand, and perched his Princess extension in their place. He proceeded to place hundreds of long distance calls to the administrative offices of various sacred denominations represented in the Salt Lake City yellow pages, inquiring as to going rates for castings-out and other such esoteric services.

Scientologists, Rosicrucians and Roman Catholics began chartering small buses out into the white desert, and challenging each other to grotesque showdowns in the purple back bedroom of the Barkdull family's modest mobile home. Such theological measures, combined with various over the-counter downers, brought my cousin a few minutes of sleep when the sun was well up and I was around to hold his shrouded hand. But, judging from Pynn's moaning dreams, it finally became obvious, even to his brain-dead father, that professional medical attention was needed, if not downright custodial care.

Papa Barkdull had no help from his wife, my auntie, Pynn's mama—the woman whom we all secretly called Death Lady. She couldn't handle any emotion other than her own barely sublimated pansexual lust, and spent all her time avoiding her unhappy son at choir practice in the local prayer hall, where she was star soprano soloist on account of her preternatural vibrato. But eventually, Papa Barkdull, unassisted, was able to convince "Crazy" Pynn that he ought to spend some time in Our Lady of Sorrows' psych ward.

"Them cat-lickers, they's used to dealin with deep feelins 'n stuff," explained Papa.

Soon, "Crazy" Pynn got bored in the pastel loony bin and started spilling his guts to the various orderlies and janitors and junkies at Our Lady's. He had a fairly horrible story to tell, which he corroborated by removing the silken gloves he'd worn ever since getting off the Greyhound.

It seemed that Pynnie's companion on the mission—a Vietnam-vet and native of this very desert, in fact, who bore the odd given name Streckfuss—had tried deliberately to drive the poor boy mad through psychological torment and even physical cruelty. Pynnie, with what seemed chillingly to resemble glee, displayed evidence of ritual scalding and shackle blisters on his body. His hands and feet looked like the Creature from the Black Lagoon's flippers, the skin melted along the phalanges and solidified in hideous brown webs of scar tissue. When pressed, however, he was unable to produce a single cigarette burn. They were Mormons, after all.

The law was called in, for even a self-effacing old desert hound-dog like Papa Barkdull couldn't overlook a disservice this blatant. They extradited Pynn's companion from Salem, where he had set up housekeeping in a seventeenth-century garret and surrounded himself with adherents to a quasi-religious sect of his own co-devising, a polygamist coven featuring old ladies and orgiastic anal rituals, Streckfuss acting as Prophet, Seer and Revelator.

The judge, in pronouncing his verdict, observed that this sort of heretical behavior was a rapidly growing trend among Mormon proselytizers throughout the world. He cited the recent misadventure of the young missionary stationed in England, who claimed to have been followed clear across the Atlantic, forcibly chained down for weeks on end, and repeatedly raped by a certain Dairy Princess from Centerville, Utah. And, when a reporter from the National Enquirer asked, "How on earth does a female rape a male? How does a man get coerced into intercourse without at least his consent, if not his cooperation?" the boy explained, "She used her mouth first." And everybody went, "Oh." Next question.

Well, the judge (not surprisingly a good Brother of the Church himself), said that he'd decided to make an example of Pynn's companion, this young Streckfuss, to put a stop to these lurid shenanigans that were interfering with God's work all across the face of the earth and so embarrassing the General Authorities. He put Streckfuss away in Utah's for-real insane asylum: not a ferny upstairs ward staffed by bleeding-heart mackerel snappers, such as the place where Pynn went, but the bona-fide, thorazine-steaming, state-run clink in the uncharted outskirts of Provo.

Actually, the depiction of "Crazy" Pynn as pure victim might have been more useful to the Barkdulls' lawyers than it was accurate. Nobody seemed to notice that Exhibit-A, the original copy of the Massachusetts coven's bizarre charter, was not only written in the "victim's" florid penmanship, but in his fancy-shmancy rhetorical style as well. Where had Pynnie gotten his webs on all that empurpled vocabulary, that architectonic syntax? From the same dark, grisly, potent place where children in exorcism movies derive their British accents, maybe?

In any case, the court elected to penalize the culprit's father as well, just for good measure. Coincidentally a "Bishop" of the church, this old gentleman was reputed to enjoy dim and peculiar ties to the Barkdull clan. (This was not all that astonishing, as everyone was dimly and peculiarly tied through plural marriage.) Streckfuss' father was forced to pay my cousin a dozen or so thousands of dollars, plus court costs. There were whisperings that the "Bishop's" elevated, yet shadowy, ranking in the sacred hierarchy had helped him get off so lightly.

With the small fortune in emotional damages, plus a couple bank loans, "Crazy" Pynn was able to open up his Hollywood Monster Hobby Shoppe in Salt Lake. It turned out to be quite a successful experiment in creative entrepreneurship. And while it stood, the Shoppe was neither bombed nor boycotted, nary a Mormon booger wiped on the plastic cobweb-festooned front window. Evidently, the "Bishop" was too ashamed, or too busy, or had simply forgotten, to wield his influence to wreak retaliation on the snitch who got his son Streckfuss in such Dutch.

In his locally famous store, "Crazy" Pynn stocked easy-to-assemble scale models of the Blob, icky rubber tarantulas, etc., all those witchy things that make children wince a bit, but don't hurt them or give bad dreams from which they can't readily awaken. My favorite retail items were the hundreds of monster masks which my cousin stacked and strung everywhere. I used to loiter near the cash register and watch these things writhe with their own animation, like a plague of toads and locusts, a spontaneous generation of morbidity.

They were the expensive kind, shaped to cover the whole head and neck, molded every conceivable vomity shade and texture, with tufts of real human hair embedded at odd spots, sprouting rankly from the sides of these disembodied noggins. The masks must have been designed by medical students with minds sickened from extended intimacy with cadavers. They looked like the portraits in the Syphilitic's Museum in Liverpool; or the pregnant corpses you can sometimes see discarded in north African mule pens; or the bubonic plague victim crumpled in the lower left cor-

101

ner of Grunewald's "Temptation of Saint Anthony," with his rictus-smile, blue epidermis, and exploding scarlet navel.

Supreme harelips throve and blossomed beyond mere oral cavities, splitting whole noses into single-nostriled tubes of plastic monster-snot. Graying, greening skin sank around empty orbits with blackened lids flapping loose. Wormlike veins erupted from the underbellies of eyeballs that hung on red strings over cheeks bursting with custardy matter. These were clinically accurate representations of the penultimate state of all flesh, the transitoriness of connective tissue, the religion-engendering horror of impermanence, caught for all eternity in non-biodegradable latex. They were time machines that gave me a look at my future self.

Here in my cuzzie's store resided timeless art that would be slippery, resilient and whole when the Isenheim Altarpiece was carbon jam between the toe-claws of some post-World War III gamma mutant. These rubbery false faces heralded the demise of Homo sapiens as a species, its mongrelization, its miscegenation, its regressive breeding into swamps and tar-pits.

Speaking of which, a certain amount of nepotism soon crept into the administration of the Hollywood Monster Hobby Shoppe. Though I hadn't quite yet fully blossomed into the magnificent stature which I enjoy today, Cousin "Crazy" Pynn came up with a way to employ the six-foot seven-inch, two-hundred-and-eighty-three-pound, fifteen-year-old me.

In response to a waking dream he experienced one afternoon in the stock room, my new boss inaugurated the very popular Marauding Beastie Service ("Hire 'em out! Scare your loved ones dead!"). He gainfully employed a downright regiment of burly, immature dope fiends such as me, a whole generation of junior Karloffs, Lugosis and Chaneys. Pynn used to pump us full of that good old-fashioned Purple Haze and make us available to working-class Mormons with poorly developed senses of humor who wanted family members traumatized. It was sort of an escort service to and from hell, and I turned out to be one of the more sought-after Frankensteins.

This job, as one may well imagine, involved the pubescent me in a zillion zany, madcap misadventures, to be sure, which I am unable recall at this very instant—except to say that the most memorable of these gigs provided me not only with my first in-person glimpse of labia minora, but also with a hairline crack in the base of my skull which still sometimes twinges a bit when I—

But, here. Allow me to demonstrate.

* * * *

I'm the patchwork corpse, jerry-rigged, galvanized, and duly dispatched by The Modern Prometheus. Layers of barf-green latex slide along cold sweat. My huge jacket smells of mothballs. I'm standing in the dark willowy back yard of a stranger's duplex, which is fastened, cystwise, halfway up the side of an oversized mountain that rims the Mormon "Zion."

The house key in my hand writhes like a centipede. Through the lace curtain I see a squared circle glowing orange and turquoise. Howard Cosell's mouth is bobbing up and down; and, coming out of his mouth, trilling, perfectly in synch, is the squeaking voice of an electric meter drilled into the red brick wall beside my ponderous green head.

I see a lady's robed legs cross and uncross in front of the TV—a Mormon plumber's mother-in-law whom I've been assigned to scare to death. If she loses control of her bladder and bowels both, there'll be a tip in it for me, and maybe even a nice bonus. Pynnie's got some Clear Light back at the shoppe. I take a growling breath—

And then, all at once, the wiseacre razzer, the color announcer to my ball game, my logorrheic consciousness, shuts up. All verbiage is cleared away from a yellow sky, for the length of time it takes to blink once.

I snap to, flat on my ass in a Doberman pinscher's horse meat-reeking supper dish, all four limbs and twenty digits cold and numb, tingling, no circulation.

Oddly, my employer, my pimp, is seated very close to me on the plumber's patio. Pynnie is adjusting the silver-painted rubber bolt that seems to be screwed into the side of my neck. He's saying, "Did you know that Death Lady wet-nursed Streckfuss?"

Before I can say "Huh?" or "Who's minding the store?" my boss cousin reaches into his pocket and produces something trim and metallic. "See my new toy?" he says, holding up a tiny piece of electronic equipment, a genuine Sony microcassette recorder. He cradles it in an ungloved web, and coos, "I'm real proud of it."

He clicks the thing on, and it makes sounds that might be tentatively identified as emanating from some sordid zoo's chimp house at feeding time. But, no, Pynn explains that the recording was made in the master bedroom of a certain particle-board mobile home in the middle of a nearby wasteland.

"I concealed this apparatus, secret and nifty, in my parents' laundry hamper," says Pynn over the ape noises. "Smell?"

It is offered up to my nose, but politely declined.

"Turn it down." I whisper. "What if the plumber's mother-in-law hears?"

"Weren't you paying attention?" snickers Pynn, turning it up. "She's already scared dead. Forget about her. Listen to your auntie and uncle instead. They're getting comfortable."

At the time this recording was made, Mama and Papa Barkdull seem to have been playing the gamy-wamies of middle-aged people who can no longer do a whole lot of bona-fide pair-bonding.

"Where'm I gonna pinch?" yowls Death Lady over the one-inch speaker dangling by a strap from her son's disfigured wrist.

"Don'tcha do that to me nope-nope-nope," replies my uncle.

"Crazy" Pynn has the whole routine committed to heart. Mr. and Mrs. Barkdull's shared moment of connubial pleasuring is preserved for posterity not only on microcassette, but in the kinesthetic memory of their sole spawn and heir. He mouths their grimaces, and pantomimes the otherwise unimaginable actions that must've produced the fleshy splorts and rubbing sounds. He throws himself into one, then the other character, like a border-line-non-compos-mentis TV comic. "Laugh at me, or I promise you I will die," he shrieks in ear-splitting body language. He squawks and squirts and grunts along with his fons et origo.

The dobie pinscher into whose supper dish my ass is wedged begins to howl and snarl from the shadows in which it is, with any luck, securely chained.

Soon enough, the locutions of my auntie and "unker," inarticulate enough under less passionate circumstances, degenerate into pure white noise. In response, Pynnie dives to his belly on the patio flagstones and slithers like a jack rabbit partly squished on a salty highway. He sizzles saliva froth all over my Frankenstein-booted insteps, and makes his beautiful golden face as ugly as the less popular monster masks, with gawks intended to impersonate each of his parents in turn.

"Cousinhood is a dangerous neighborhood," says Leo Tolstoy, but in a different context.

Pynnie even looks up once and shoots me a chillingly accurate imitation of the trademark sneer which Death Lady produces while soloing at Sunday meetings in the prayer hall, a rictus of greasy rut that nearly puts the fear in me. He shoves a few fused fingers into the corners of his rosebud mouth and yanks masochistically down.

"Isn't this almost too disgusting?" he laughs, and snaps the microcassette recorder off just as my uncle starts making ejaculation sounds. Pynn gets up off this perfect stranger's patio, sets his hair straight, and dusts himself off.

At this point I feel I simply must demur. From between my brown-painted cadaver-lips I say, "But, Pynnie, Those sorts of gamy-wamies are what made you."

After a stunned pause, he murmurs, "Sweet Jesus, I never thought of it that way." He hunkers back down next to me, and tries to say more, but his voice cracks. He turns and looks, glassy-eyed, at his reflection in the doggy's water dish, then at his shiny red shoes.

"You have a cousin," Pynn says absently. "I mean besides me. An honorary cousin, I should say. Not a blood cousin, but a milk cousin. Suckled at the same blessed paps that suckled me. Did you know? My former missionary companion? Streckfuss?"

"Stop lying."

Pynn gives off a look of offended piety.

"Tell the truth," I say.

Pynn takes on a homiletical tone of voice. "What a 'Bishop' wants," he informs me, "a 'Bishop' gets."

"And he wanted your hideous mom's nipple sauce curdling in his only son's belly?"

"It's well-known fact. Local lore. If you didn't spend all your time hulking around Gomorrah in full make-up, you'd already know this."

"Well, yeah. But rental tits? I thought that was just way down south, back in the old days, with former slaves—I mean, you know."

Pynn leans against the plumber's fly-screened porch door and says, "Are you ready to hear what that old hireling milch-cow used to do to the 'Bishop's' boy? I remember this, even though I was just a small child myself, because she always made me watch and even assist sometimes. You know the old line: 'Hand me the Handi-Wipes, Pynnie, our wee-wee Streckie-boy spilled!'

"You see, she had contractually obligated herself to the most powerful Mormon around, but Mama was too busy with sacred church work and choir practice to fix the baby solid food, So she kept him nursing far beyond the weaning time prescribed by our northern industrialized culture. This had the added advantage of extending the pay period. Plus she liked the twitches it gave her uterus to have a little man tugging away at her areolae. 'Tightens me up for your ol' Papa's salami,' is what she used to sizzle in my face as she suckled the customer, and I couldn't figure out what in the world she was talking about, lunch or what?

106

"And li'l Streckums was thinking about lunch, too. He was a growing boy, hungry for some solid meat for his bones and muscles to develop on. Sometimes he forgot himself, lulled two-thirds unconscious by the breast anyway, and he sank his razor-sharp rattler teeth into the Death Lady.

"And she screamed the filthiest words I have ever heard. She never, ever swore other times, because she was such a good religious woman, the first-string soprano soloist in the prayer hall choir. But at feeding time it was 'Why, you filthy li'l rim-jobbing, smegma-gulping clit-twirler!' And she raked my future missionary companion's cheek with her fingernails until he opened his mouth to cry and she could slide her teat back out to the safety of her under-wire bra, bleeding, and that would be the end of Streckfuss' nurture for that particular day.

"She'd supplement this jejune diet with saltine crackers. That was his only solid food besides wrinkled dug-flesh, and he'd only get them when Mommy was sure he was cutting a new tooth, a ragged hole in his gums. He would jam that salt cracker in his little rosebud mouth, my client baby brother, and scream in agony, but couldn't stop chewing because he was so ravenous. And mama would watch with no expression at all on her face. Sometimes she'd press a hand or two between her thighs and glance at me.

"She'd pump the stranger full to bursting with that awful red sugar-water from a baby bottle. Then she'd swathe her head in a brown terrycloth imitation animal hide with bottle caps tinkling all over it, and prance around our mobile home, making noises and faces intended to mock our daddy, who was out steadfastly operating his backhoe somewhere in the wilderness. And she'd make my baby un-brother laugh and laugh until he peed that red sugar water all over his diapers. And then she would encourage me to help her heap scorn on Strecky-Wee-Wee for being a pants-pissing baby, followed by more salty things for the wounds in his mouth. 'Breakfast for Streckfuss! Breakfast for Streckfuss!' she'd warble at full vibrato.

107

"And when he got constipated from all this malnutrition and turmoil, Mommy sodomized our patron's son with a Vaseline-coated pencil eraser. 'To get them ding-dang contractions going,' is what she explained while making me watch.

"You know, just the standard behavior that females engage in whenever we're haplessly placed in their charge, the basic mewling and puking stuff, the usual monster-making that only a poorly toilet-trained fag like me and a connoisseur of unattractiveness like you would care to bring up in polite company.

"She used to walk bare-naked in front of my li'l Streckums and me. She'd scratch herself and bend over, pretending to pick up something. She'd have us lie in bed with her and play rub-the-backs. Neither of us learned to wipe our bummy properly until seventh or eighth grade, and only then by trial and error, 'cause Mama always did it for us. She deliberately misinformed us just to see our little eyes widen in amazement: she told us that the daddy peed in the mommy's belly button and then there was a baby. And she'd massage her bosoms like we weren't there, cuz. She used to have us three bathe together, me and my pseudo-sibling and her. And, pretending to teach us personal hygiene, she'd pull our foreskins, which were never removed like all the other boys' in gym class. She swore up and down it was for laudable anti-Semitic reasons, but it was actually just so she could tweak them twice a week for nearly a decade and a half. That's why she named me, her first-born, like she did. You know, to sound like 'penis'? I, at least, must have enjoyed it, because I always called, 'Mama, will you bring me a towel?' clear up until I was seventeen, even after she'd stopped pulling my pynnie 'cause I was a man with hair of my own and she was religious and in the choir. She's the soprano soloist, you know? First string, of the whole prayer house choir? I think that shows a certain amount of serious application, don't you?"

He looked imploringly out of the corner of one eye.

For some peculiar reason of my own, I suddenly felt like laughing in my cousin's face. But I didn't. That would be cruel—but not cruel enough. Not for the Marauding Beastie, not tonight. So, instead of laughing, I delved deep into myself and conjured up an ultimately cynical, latently queer notion to utter in an undead voice, to make things even more difficult for my poor blood-cuzzie. I loved this guy, always had. But, you know, what the hell?

"Pynnie," I said, taking the golden forearm and gazing into the clear, bewildered eyes. "We are all of us sprung from feces. We are like those mushrooms I got growing in my bathroom: rank things, sprouted temporarily in a hard white place that was intended just for defecation."

I was about to add, "We're just waiting in this laundry hamper of an earth for a giant angel to come pluck and gobble us for his own recreational purposes, which have nothing to do with us as persons," or something anticlimactic like that—but, at that moment, Pynn's thumb made a little spasm and flipped on the Sony microcassette recorder, just long enough for us two tall youngsters to hear the splatter and plop of Mama Barkdull's cackling, orgasming and singing the first few bars of "Whoa Promise Me."

"Shit is what we're sprung from," I insisted. "Unlovely and unloving shit."

"I know," choked Pynn in despair.

I celebrated this conceit, and such a pithy, almost aphoristic expression thereof, with a few death-embracing lungfuls of the most common combustion-supportive air pollutant in modern urban zones, adulterated liberally with the world's major greenhouse gas.

As for Pynn, he actually started crying. Quiet sighs and hiccoughs. Catching his tears like little black lagoons in the webs of either hand, and wiping them away, bravely, like a sad, pretty girl, he cried, Pynnie did. And I felt like a hireling mutant whore.

"I'm sorry."

"I know," repeated Pynnie, much more firmly. "It's okay." He understood, better than most people would. He smiled, and offered me a tiny windowpane, a bonus.

Bachelor Biff and His Foo-Chow Whore Get a Crypto-Missionary in Big Trouble with the Chi-Coms

An unmarried man over the age of nineteen is a danger to society.
—Brigham Young

On the rim of a bay in the South China Sea, the proprietor of Telestial Deep Sea Fishing Expeditions Co., Inc., was ensconced in his villa-style courtyard that doubled as an open-air rumpus room.

This man was called, of course, LaMar, and he was delighted to be surrounded by beanbags and bongo boards, exploded pomegranates and his pregnant wife, who flopped among the honeysuckle trellises planted instead with peas (security against the Armageddon that his religion had plagiarized from actual Christians).

Tykes swarmed everywhere, a jumbo-sized passel of once-every-year-and-a-half kids, all blond. They strangled each other with the red neckerchiefs of the communist Young Pioneers, which had been misrepresented as scholastic achievement awards in the press back home. The youngsters were too many to count. Mommy evidently short-shrifted each of them in the breast milk department, the better to get an early start on the next, according to the immemorial custom of their 160-year-old faith. Green Jello with tiny marshmallows was the Similac of this household.

This was the sort of domestic scene that requires great temerity and a strong stomach to infiltrate—the very qualities which Bachelor Biff positively oozed, for he was a self-starting kind of guy (given a small nudge from the local power structure). And LaMar seemed willing to semi-welcome Biff, for the moment at least, as a misguided tourist, accompanied by an evidently ungravid, therefore unimportant, female. In fact, the whole family, following the lead of their patriarch, looked askance on Biff's "wife" at first.

"She's over twelve and under fifty-five," they whispered to one another. "So where's her dacron-polyester maternity outfit at?"

Then Biff realized that he hadn't presented his credentials yet. The words of the prophet Brigham Young denouncing all wifeless men as dangers to society still rang fresh in Mormon ears; and, for all LaMar knew, the two of them could just have been a pair of unmarried adventurists looking for a free feed, trying to impose themselves in the name of compatriotism.

So Biff flashed his "Temple Recommend" (forged by one of the more compliant calligraphers this side of the Yangtze River), and began, in medias res, to tell rehearsed lies in a creditable Latter-Day-Saint accent.

"Golly-dang, LaMar. I and the little missus are wrapping up a two-year proselytizing mission. Hushy-hush, of course. You know how these Maoists are."

LaMar couldn't help but roll his eyes in sympathetic exasperation and say, "Oppressive totalitarian regime with contempt for human rights such as freedom of religion."

"Yeah," said Biff. "Stuff like that."

"And which of our many fine seminaries were you dispatched from?" asked LaMar, starting to smile in a friendly way.

Biff thought fast and said, "Um...the one in Salt Lake City?"

He risked incurring Babylon-fear in exchange for the near certainty that this obvious Provo partisan wouldn't know anybody in such a decadent sinkhole.

LaMar looked sad. "Oh, well. Lots of Tongan converts up there, playing softball and eating Shetland ponies." It was as if Biff had said he was from Iceland.

But there was a way to get past the mistrust. Biff made a gesture of the head, a wordless, Reaganesque nod, signifying, "Gee, I'd really like to talk to you...alone."

111

He suffused it with the slightest lip- and eyelid-pouting fluidity, just enough below-the-waistband appeal to make the request for a private audience irresistible to someone who would rather spread his genetic material thinly over an obscene number of tiny carcasses than admit he'd experienced some variant impulses inside his human pants.

So the two men headed out together for the porch and the sooty sea panorama it afforded, leaving their better halves to stare at each other in repulsed silence while the freckled kindergarten shrieked around their feet.

"Don't nod off till I get us established or you can kiss off the fucking bonus," Biff hissed to his "wife" in Foo-Chow gutter dialect as he passed grinning out of the rumpus room. Evidently it had been beyond the capability of the Public Security Bureau to dig him up a floozy without a severe opiate addiction.

LaMar was on the topic of sex before the screen door could shut. "Flip!" he whispered in a croaking falsetto. "My LurBobbie hasn't touched a Tampax since we got hitched in the Temple!"

This was too easy. Without burning any calories at all, Biff heard himself reply, "Well, I haven't even had a chance to baptize my wife yet. And the only reason she hasn't touched a Tampax is that none of them ever do."

He waved his arm out across the town-encrusted foothills, to make it clear who "them" might be, and continued. "Gol, LaMar, we been married three weeks already and she's not even, um, you know—"

"You bet," said LaMar before the naughty word could be spoken. His face wore an expression of condescension disguised as commiseration, as if to say, "Serves you right for intermarrying, doesn't it? As if the world needs more hybrids. But, considering your point of origin, I guess I can't blame you. From what I've heard it's well-nigh impossible to unearth a virgin in that Gomorrah-on-the-Dead-Sea."

There was a moment of silence for Biff to repent of his own poor judgment. In deep sadness, he scanned the nearly deserted waterway of this languishing Special Economic Zone.

"Of course," he moaned after an appropriate while. "You're right. Too bad I don't have several little sons to share your wisdom with."

Childlessness in a coreligionist, along with all its political implications, would certainly seep into LaMar's secret dewy places—especially here in the land of the one-child policy. Biff glanced at his host's trouser-bulge with wistful, younger-brotherly admiration. That would give him a feeling of alpha-male superiority, which might lead to even more fundamental indiscretion.

"By the way, Brother LaMar, are you with The Company?"

"You mean the Bonneville Corporation?" He smiled smugly, arched his back and bounced on the balls of his feet. "Well, Telestial Deep Sea Fishing Expeditions Co., Inc., has received some financial backing in exchange for—"

"No, no, no." Biff oozed a little closer on the veranda, in a splash of poinsettia-haunting lizards with green suction cups for toes. He whispered, in a babyish voice, "The Company. You kno-o-o-ow!"

"You bet!" chuckled LaMar, displaying two huge upper incisors.

Did people from anyplace else say you bet? Utah, the You Bet State.

"That's a secret, m'kay? But, seeing as how you're a good brother of the church and all, well—" He smirked a bit, surveyed the bay with crinkled eyes, and spilled his guts. It was almost more than Biff cared to hear.

"I'm just a minor operative, keeping a secret tally of the comings and goings of boats like that one there."

He pointed out across the harbor in a non-specific way useless to Biff, who was trying to align his nose with the blond forearm, when LurBobbie, or whatever her name was, appeared toting a couple huge bowls and a half-gallon of something with

113

green and white stripes. She'd probably chosen to break it out at this early hour as an excuse to leave the rumpus room/courtyard for a breath of air, away from Biff's opium-scented traveling companion. The label on the carton seemed to say Dental Cream Swirl Frozen Dessert Product.

"Shipped just a whole bunch of miles by diplomatic pouch," beamed LaMar.

"Gol, Lammy!" she giggled before demurely excusing herself and withdrawing. "You're not supposed to tell nobody."

When she was gone and they could resume talking man-to-man, LaMar forked over a pair of binoculars and said, "That's a cadre out of Vladivostok, here for some kind of high-level lefty shenanigans nobody knows about. See? You can tell it's a Roosky craft by how tacky the skipper is dressed. Like Pete Seeger."

"Flip!" cried Biff. "All he needs is a banjo."

"When the wind's just right for our little backyard sound dish to operate efficiently, you can hear that most of the tunes they play on their cheap Hong Kong ghetto blaster are in minor keys. That's a dead giveaway. Nobody but a morbid polar totalitarian would prefer that sound. Except for 'May there Always Be Mommy,' which they play occasionally. I kind of like that one. It's probably on their tape by mistake."

"A pirating error," sniffed Biff, wondering vaguely if he'd ever heard a tune by that name.

"Yeah," giggled LaMar, who was really loosening up now. He began to get a little theatrical, mocking their accents as he spoke. "They love Ze Bittles and Aunty Villiams." He held out both hands and signaled for Biff to join him in a mock group-sing, which Biff did, once he'd caught the gist:

Ve had choy
Ve had fan
Ve had sissons in the sun
La-la-la...

114

Then LaMar caught hold of himself before too much pro-
fane hilarity could seep into the conversation. He began to look a
little guilty for crooning a secular song on a Sunday afternoon. As
if in compensation, he got even more maudlin than he was accusing his seagoing adversaries of being.

"After a while eavesdropping tends to, um, sort of human-
ize these people," he said, tentatively; and when Biff conjured up
his most horrified gasp, LaMar hastily added, "But not enough to
endanger our national interests, you know, Brother—um, Brother—?"

Biff pretended to be unwilling to reveal his secret
name-in-religion to a potential turncoat, a fence-straddler. Almost
in despair (would this be reported to his neighborhood Bishop back
in Provo?), LaMar tried to redeem himself by casting further as-
persions across the waves.

"You can also tell Sovietsky yachts because, while the other foreign pleasure cruisers have your half-nak—um, well,
half-undressed skinny young girls, the Rooskies prefer your
chunky fifty-year-olds in black rubber one-pieces."

At the mention of the word "rubber," LaMar got slightly
out of control. He sputtered, "And all of them, male and female,
got fifty percent rag bond-white skin and juicy Khrushchev warts
nestled in the crannies of their faces between vodka-pickled skin
flaps, like this—"

He reached up and wrenched a Gogol grimace out of his
face. He inserted thumbs up both nostrils and dragged down his
lower lip and eyelids with the other fingers, in the efficient manner
of fourth graders that Biff had never quite mastered, though not for
lack of earnest effort.

Then LaMar seemed to realize he was being infantile. He
switched gears once more, this time into a more somber speed.

"But I suppose that, hard-pressed, the prophet Brigham
Young would've admitted our Slavic brethren to the elevated ranks
of the White and Delightsome, huh?"

Biff let loose a burst of air, deftly dissipating all tension, and said, "Gosh, I never thought of it that way. But, I guess so!"

He glanced meaningfully back through the matrixed gnats of the screen door at his high-yellow "wife," who'd dozed off despite the warning and was sprawled in the middle of the floor with her legs wide apart.

But LaMar didn't get it. He thought Biff's glance was intended to switch topics from pale Russians to tan Chinese. He said, "I fig they're fixing to fall back into the hug of the polar bear. Just look around you at these docks, spanking new and completely idle. Modernization is a failure. So it's hi-hi Roosky-wooskies! Scarlet monolith time!" He actually pinched Biff's ass.

"Flip, LaMar," croaked Biff, trying his best to gag down the old primordial sodomite-horror which, in his case, manifested itself in elevator stomach. Undercover intelligence work is a bleak and sordid business.

LaMar got close and whispered breathlessly up against his withering earlobe. "I'll tell you a secret if you promise not to tell anybody, not even the old ball and chain, m'kay?"

"M'kay."

By this point, LaMar had entered into that talkative mood peculiar to Mormons who, by some clerical error or ill-considered board decision, have been allowed access to sensitive information. (And there are lots of them; the U.S. intelligence community is bottom-heavy with Latter-Day Saints.) It had taken so much effort for LaMar's Heavenly Father-blasted brain to absorb this data that, in order to call it back up, he was obliged to allow his personality, such as it was, to be subsumed, so as to make room. He was doing an impression of an Associated Press Wire Service machine.

"Did you know the Soviets nuked Xinjiang in the early sixties? Yup! Forty thousand dead, but they were just your Uighur nomads and other Turkic types, your brownish little Allah-babbling tribesmen and like that, so Beijing didn't get too ticked, except for the face-loss deal, don't you know. It was just a

116

tank-deployed tactical weapon. I saw the seismic reports at Brigham Young University. Flip these socialists, you know?"

What security problem? thought Biff. *Our country's got a security problem?*

"Yeah-boy," he marveled aloud, carelessly slipping a Mayberryism among the Utahisms. "Wouldn't that be a tale to tell your blue-eyed son as he sat on your knee in front of the fireplace?"

That got this Latter-Day Saint right where he lived. For the first time he looked directly on Biff as another sentient organism.

"To what degree in the Melchizedek Rite have you attained, Brother?"

Boy, oh boy: more Mormon lore, from a level even a post-DeVoto expert like Biff hadn't bothered to penetrate. He drew a complete blank and had to fake it.

"I'm lax. I'm remiss, Brother LaMar. Please forgive me."

"That's all right. Don't feel badly. Since we've been cast together on this remote shore and you have displayed such a right-minded attitude toward everything, I think that I might see my way clear to initiating you into some of the higher mysteries of our Melchizedek Order—um, perhaps in return for services rendered?"

Suddenly, as if on cue, from behind Biff's shoulder came the semi-articulated belching noises of LurBobbie. She was requesting the withdrawal of her larger sons from between the knees of his comatose bride.

Biff felt the millstone dragging him down already, small intestines first. He asked himself, deep in his heart, "Do I really want to buy into this sort of thing that badly?"

"No!" screamed the Me Generationist inside him, "No!"

But there was something round and solid about the youngest one still on the tit, the one who hadn't quite walked or talked or swallowed the Heavenly Father puke yet. It charmed Bachelor Biff's dream-self, and also scared the shit out of him in an ambiguous way that resembled nothing he'd ever experienced. He decided to think of it, tentatively at least, as the indeterminateness of real life, and try to let it go at that for the time being.

But why the sheer numbers of little lumps of indeterminateness? Two or three, or just one, seemed reasonable even to the territorial beast that snarled in him.

Then he noticed something proprietary, like a cross between the leer of the butcher and the pimp, in the gloating look LaMar sent forth whenever he patted a few of his spawn on the heads or asses. Biff had lived among these people for whole sad chunks of his life, and had unwillingly driven through minuscule towns like Lehi, Utah, where two-thirds of the population had been implicated in the organized mix-'n-match/swap meet-style sexual molestation of their own children.

LurBobbie belched again.

Nausea and the flight impulse nearly overtook Biff's sense of duty. Somehow, he maintained enough presence to choke out the words, "S-s-services rendered? Well, um... Gol-dang, you just name it, Bro!"

"There are several Palestinians abiding in your neck of the woods, I'm told. Scholarshipped medical students chained to a conveyor belt in the municipal abortion mill."

Biff's jaw went slack with release of tension and hung down as the rest of his body soared with the angels. It seemed the Latter-Day Saint wanted a camel jock or two to service LurBobbie, not a coreligionist. Biff emitted an inconclusive schwa sound, which was misinterpreted as affirmation.

"Well," said LaMar, "you could sort of buddy-wuddy it up to these Philistines. It's not supposed to be all that difficult. Sure, they want to see Americans hemorrhaging in the sand with their noses slit up the side and all that; but when it gets down to practicalities, these little goat-hubbies usually turn out to have a sentimental admiration for us, which can be manipulated into the kind of emotional attachment that lends itself to major indiscretion." He rolled his eyes, clucked his tongue and moved closer. "You could

118

just, you know, report back to me occasionally on your little P.L.O.-buddies' thought processes. Simple as pie. M'kay?"

Biff was so busy analyzing his attitudes toward his own Judeo-Christian background that he didn't hear that last "M'kay?" and said nothing in reply.

"Very good, a silent consent. With a little practice you could go to work for The Company—and I don't mean Telestial Deep Sea Fishing Expeditions Co., Inc."

LaMar made a move to pinch some ass again, which, even in his reverie, Biff was able gently but firmly to repulse.

"Oh, that's right. We're into serious business now," said LaMar, swallowing a smirk. "Melchizedek stuff. M'kay. Now, the higher Priesthood does have some amazing capabilities in the promotion of fertility, as you can plainly see. As a matter of fact, some of our techniques, which date way, way back to the early days in Nauvoo, Illinois, share a broad archetypal and conceptual base with the splinter-Taoist semen retention isometrics as practiced by the aboriginals of the southern Thai mountain ranges and—um, did you say your wife hadn't been baptized?"

Biff oozed out a sheepish, self-castigating kind of moan.

"Well, then! Let's all board my boat, both our houses, my future fellow patriarch, and sail to a select spot in this oriental ocean. I shall show you some deep secrets of the White Salamander Brotherhood and provide you with a foolproof fertility amulet and rite, all combined with a bona-fide full-immersion baptism for your lovely life-mate. You'll be in possession of a fetal Biffy, Jr., within the month, I guarantee. Sort of a celestial package deal."

* * * *

So everybody, tykes included, wallowed out into green fluid and splashed away until everything began to get orangish and darkish, and they anchored off a desolate island, which the whore kept eyeing with definite revulsion, as if she knew something about the place Biff didn't.

They underwent a kind of plagiarized Freemasonry-type bare-naked fertility rite involving fervid prayer-in-tongues, the donning and doffing of the secret white Temple garments, and LurBobbie's marshmallow-palms cupping Biff's testicles on deck while the dumbfounded little prostitute had to go swimming with LaMar.

Before her head was pushed under, while trying to scratch LaMar's radiant eyes out of their sockets and kick his balls under the water, she shrieked three syllables of gutter dialect. Biff took the requisite full minute and a half of her total submersion to recognize this word: it could be rendered literally in English as "finger-droppers," and signified, for Christ's sake, lepers. And he realized they were floundering within sneezing distance of an isolation colony.

LaMar came spouting up and trod water for a while, mumbling a benediction on his new proselyte—for she was his, not Biff's convert, though Biff had been the one to unearth her. She would go on LaMar's tally sheet in the great Up Yonder and get him gold stars off his neighborhood Bishop back in Provo. Red Chinks were at a premium these days, what with the "open door policy" and the crack at tithing a quarter of the known universe's population of economic animals.

LaMar followed Biff's gaze to the questionable shoreline and volunteered some more information.

"I'm told that place used to veritably flutter with tens of thousands of beautiful egrets. Now the islanders outnumber any other life form."

The leprous types had already gathered on their diesel-grimy beach to observe the small devotional service by moonlight. Some of the weller ones waded out a few feet into the gray surf. Biff saw gritty waves abrading sallow calves and ankles, taking a mushy toll.

He risked blowing his cover by politely demurring when LaMar intoned a solemn request for him to disengage his shriveling scrotum from LurBobbie's pudgy grasp and join his newly reborn, newly eternalized spouse in God's boundless baptismal font, or something like that.

"The natives are friendly," said LaMar, by way of persuasion. "See how they light our way with the torches of brotherhood? If your baptism quota hasn't been filled after these two years in Red purgatory—and I have a suspicion it might not be, Brother Biffy, seeing how your own wife is just now entering into the Kingdom of Bliss—you wouldn't be imprudent to consider dog-paddling over there later on tonight and dunking a few devils. They look ripe for the picking."

Biff must've been getting tired and incautious. He made the obvious tithing joke about impecunious Hansen's disease patients: single digits per annum, and so on. It was met with an outright suspicious silence from the patriarch and his whole caterwauling clan. There was a pause, and Biff had made it, at least, pregnant.

This was not the first time his piety had come into question today. But Utahns are famed the world over for their gullibility. Deng Xiaoping once sent a couple of his desert-reclamation men to Provo to fetch a bunch of Mo-mo dowsing experts back to drought-struck Xinjiang, under strict orders not to smirk when promising "an atmosphere of free trade and economic cooperation." So Biff figured his latest gaffe could be smoothed over, albeit with a drastic action: a suicidal strip of the Temple garments and a plunge into the piss-warm South China Sea. He came up gagging among bathtub toy-like sacramental paraphernalia.

Better to risk leprosy germs floating up one's butt than to blow this whole assignment, lose the favor of the Chi-Coms, and be sent back to rot behind the podium in the EFL classroom. Junky flat-backers and hyperfecundant Utahns were not ideal company, but they beat the hell out of students.

And so, the sins of the tiny oppressed worker-girl were washed away in the yeasty waters off the Special Economic Zone, while her red eyeballs floated uncomprehendingly in a vapor of stale opium. And one might suppose that the Spirit of the Lord descended upon, if not frankly mounted her at one point or another in

121

the evening. But there was no way of verifying this, for, in her idiolect and in the jargon of her trade, there were no words to express such a notion.

During the entire orgy, little blond apes skittered in and out of the yacht's turquoise superstructure, fighting over the ample contents of the bulging Toshiba fridge and eyeing coolly the various sets of multi-racial adult genitalia, which flopped on deck and floated in the inky and lumpy sea.

"JazMynne, honey, could you go back inside and close the hatch now, sweetie?" piped the mommy in her buttery mezzo-soprano. "And take little Nilla with you? Thank yo-o-o-o-o-u! We call that one Nilla 'cause it's her favorite kind."

Having said that, LurBobbie took a belly flop right into the midst of the celebrants. The little whore eyed her huge boobs in puzzlement as they wobbled lopsidedly in the fluid like downed, mismatched zeppelins.

The kids went back under duress, whining, "When we going back to 'merica? There's nothing but poot-cakes on television here!"

When it was over, closing prayers groaned, the boat started puffing up a good head of steam on the way back to the harbor, under the competent pilotage of Dorcas or JonBenet or Krystle or one of the other ambulatory spawn. The grownups dried off in the cabin and enjoyed the latest Donny and Marie Family Home Evening video, followed by Marie's workout tape for expectant mothers.

The whole time Biff's bride was either nodding off or sneaking into the head for a few tokes. He was expected to palm her little black pewter canister pipe on demand. She would come out all warm and sort of bony-cuddly, and she'd try to imitate Mrs. LaMar like a chihuahua flattering a walrus. In her longing to enjoy a few last minutes of domesticity, the whore attempted to play and snuggle with a few of the Mo-mo kids who were small and unindoctrinated enough not to have contempt for her slanted eyes. She revealed the depth of her maternal instinct by calming the fussiest suckling infant with an oily bolus of poppy tar slipped between its boneless gum and lip.

Biff put the kibosh on that, with the only means he could think of on such short notice: a diversionary tactic. His lunge for LurBobbie's hubcap-sized nipple was met with "Why didn't you do that at prayer meeting, Bro? Too late now! And you can tell your bride to keep the chocolate, thanks. We don't start them on that till they're weaned."

In other words, things had settled down to normal for an evening of socializing among American expatriates in China.

Biff chose this moment to sidle up to the gracious host—one last time, thank God. He steeled himself and intoned seductively, "Gol, Brother LaMar. The last time they shook down my prayer closet, the darn Public Security Bureau confiscated my Book of Mormon and my Pearl of Great Price and my Doctrine and Covenants."

"My goodness, all three?" He seemed genuinely concerned. "You know what they say about a Latter-Day Saint without his Three Good Tomes?"

"Yup, I know: 'He's naked already.'"

"Oh, why won't they let us get on with it and fetch souls to Heavenly Father?" cried LaMar. "It's not like as though we're superstitious self-fricasseeing heathens like the Foo Long Bing Bong, or whatever."

"Yeah," said Biff. "Um, anyways... Do you happen to have extra copies I could borrow? My own were red leather bound, of course, with the raised spine—"

"A dead giveaway."

"Yes, that's quality binding. But the missus and I'd be mighty grateful even for some dog-eared paperback editions. I have a lot of work to do with this little lady, to strengthen her position within the fold."

Biff looked fondly down at his spouse, whose few brunette pubes were evidently starting to itch, even through the narcotic that polluted her bloodstream.

LaMar stood watching her scratch for a full minute, then said, "Well, you know, Brother, I am a businessman. I'm not one of you heroic underground trench-fighters, whom I admire so deeply. To wangle my invitation from the central authorities, I had to sign an agreement promising not to proselytize, distribute tracts, or even hold Family Home Evening out on my veranda with my own kids, if you can feature that—on pain of strappado, followed by summary deportation."

Biff made his face fall to belly button-level.

"But," LaMar continued magnanimously, "since you are already a good brother of the church, well, sir—"

He opened up a sea chest brimming with scripture.

Biff beamed, "Wonderful! Say, could you inscribe the books to my wife? The dedication of a full-blown Melchizedek is not without value in the spirit world. And she's going to need all the points she can get. In Chinese, please, so she can appreciate it."

And LaMar, proprietor of Telestial Deep Sea Fishing Expeditions Co., Inc., grandly obliged, filling in the date, the place, and his own full legal name, in the boxy yet studiedly legible calligraphy of the outlander.

* * * *

After they'd come ashore and fondly parted company, Biff pledging to deliver Palestinian guts on a silver salver A.S.A.P., the damp couple took their solitary way into the foothills, smoking like mismatched chimneys. Their provincial government-provided Red Flag limousine was waiting. The moment Biff's weight hit the shock absorbers, the venerable V-8 started up with a joyous roar.

Before the pipe could completely dull her brain once again, Biff turned to the Foo-Chow whore and told her, "Next time there's a shakedown on Stalin Square, let the cops confiscate these three books and they'll leave your scumbags and cigarettes alone."

Boomtown Roosky Sing this Song

A Hiroshima city bus, marked RADIATION EFFECTS RESEARCH FOUNDATION in both Japanese and English, worms its way in low gear, sliding up inside acid rain-ravaged bamboo groves on a dank mountain that blots the sunrise from Ground Zero every morning: a sinister peak of pre-rational alchemy plunked down, among rumors of genetic engineering run amok, at the edge of a necessarily modern metropolis.

All but one of the passengers are townies, *hibakushas*—those unlucky Hiroshimites who were within a kilometer of the epicenter at the wrongest possible time, and must, twice yearly, for the rest of their lives, report to the to the labs on top of this mountain, to be prodded and skewered, solely for the selfless sake of increasing mankind's store of knowledge. No healing is done up here; otherwise, the joint would lose its funding as a pure research institution.

The bus empties out near the main entrance of the Radiation Effects Research Foundation. The bomb victims file into a large corrugated aluminum structure, a Quonset hut-like affair, unrebuilt since Douglas MacArthur's GHQ tossed it up a few weeks after the brimstone chastisement of the Hiroshimites. Everybody, save one (and a very large one at that), disappears behind flapping doors marked with bold polyglot signs:

LIVER BIOPSIES
BLOOD SCREENINGS
FOETAL TISSUE SAMPLES
    viable
    aborted
    problematic

125

STOOLS
   formed
   unformed
URINE

The sole straggler, an outsized American named Sam Edwine, wanders bravely out back and approaches a second metal
structure. It is rumored that a certain ex-Soviet witch, if not her
bubbling cauldron, can usually be located here.

This dive is marked by a rectangle of gray cloth with three
brownish words scrawled on it:

RADIATION EFFECTS CAFETERIA

In order to attain the Ray Conniff-hissing entryway, Sam is
forced to pick and cringe his way through a medical wasteland: a
forest of grandma-headed mops planted in buckets of chlorinated
rinse-water like crucifixes in jars of piss; a maze of garage
door-sized sheaves of exposed X-ray film, warping and flaking in
the green dew that drains, like peritonitis fluid, from the withered
fronds of barren date palms.

Stooping inside, he scans the rows of pastel aluminum ta-
bles, and has little difficulty picking out his mark from among her
lab-coated colleagues. She's the only one waving a bottle of
cut-rate Choya plum wine in his direction.

Valentina is fleshy and, one would suppose, more-or-less
voluptuous, at least according to the lights of men more emotionally developed than most far-western Americans: big protuberant
breasts, wide hips and a round, pale face suffused with a shrewd-
ness seen infrequently in Sam's corner of the world; and, true to
type, the sadness, the eyes gazing off into the clouds after some
lost memory of haunts less gelid.

With no preliminaries, Sam establishes his phony journalis-
tic credentials by turning his pockets inside out and allowing his
cub-reporter paraphernalia to tumble helter-skelter into space. A

126

precious microcassette recorder splorts down onto a trencher of the house specialty, cold instant macaroni and cheese, which Valentina has evidently taken the liberty of ordering on the interviewer's behalf.

As he folds himself into one of those form-fitting plastic chairs found usually in bowling alleys, Sam's massive kneecaps jostle the table. Clunking noises issue from the fist-loads of opaque, jawbreaker-sized ice cubes, which are stacked like kiddy blocks inside a couple of the Mason jars that pass, here at the Radiation Effects Cafeteria, as wine glasses.

His assignment: invite himself to the foundation on the pretext of interviewing this creature for a non-existent weekly back in old Salt Lake City (assuming Russkies still consider themselves exotic enough in the free world to make the request for such an audience seem plausible).

"Just feel her out," he was told. (Not "up," mind you.) "There could be a free lunch and drinks in it."

Valentina starts feeding her face, without a word. Disdaining chopsticks, she digs her aluminum spoon out of an old Kunming batik bag and grasps it like a cement trowel. She makes no use of her presumably opposable thumb, but sticks it out straight to nudge her left nostril with each bite, as if to flaunt her proletarian credentials.

Even the more recent snapshots of her grandchildren have a yellowish, dog-eared look when she gruffly deals them out like pinochle cards across the table, not troubling to avoid the ketchup puddles.

"A budding anarchist, that one," she growls, finally breaking the silence. She thumps the face of a red-haired picturebook fairy perched on a cast-iron trike in the snow. "But very clever."

Valentina must strain her deep contralto to be heard over the chaos of the other international biophysicists' feeding—a real chore for her. She obviously prefers to speak in a profound-sounding murmur, all ears cocked toward her.

127

"The words 'amoebic dysentery' seem not to be in his physiological vocabulary," she observes, out of nowhere.

"Huh?" Sam says, still looking at her grandchild's picture. "Whose—?"

"You know who I am talking about."

Sam follows her eyes across the cafeteria. Using a Morinaga candy bar, a lab assistant who looks distressingly like Jerry Lewis tantalizes and coaxes someone into a scary-looking, chrome-bristling back room. Bawling for the sweetie is a blackened and bent native, a locally famous river hobo, dressed in frayed polyester golfing attire, several sizes too large and a few decades out of fashion. Rumor maintains this small monster was in his mother's belly at the moment of the glamorous detonation.

Valentina says, "That particular pinhead lives on a raft in the river, and virtually subsists on raw sewage. If you're looking for some evidence of mutation, tag a few of his leukocytes and trail them like rafts through his bloodstream."

Her own genetic material having been scrambled during two helicopter rides over Chernobyl, Valentina was inspired, by way of saintly commiseration, to lend her gifts to this august institution. That's the Roosky party line. But the word around the so-called "intelligence" community is that this babushka is interested less in the wretches' irradiated chromosomes than their white blood cells. She's supposedly been pumping them full of human immunodeficiency virus and requisitioning whole quarts of serum from their veins in the name of HIV research. One's most extravagant paranoia might not be far off the mark. After all, the race to cure AIDS has taken on all the glamour of the race to the moon.

The pseudo-interviewer is temporarily speechless at the sheer creeping horror of this situation he's bumbled into. But he realizes that he can do no better than to continue the investigation, as craftily as possible under the circumstances.

"Tagging leukocytes, oh yeah," he says through a yawn, feigning boredom, inspecting a surfboard-sized thumbnail, swirling plum wine around the crusty screw-top of his Mason jar.

He obviously hasn't a clue how to go about this subtle sort of interrogation. He's got no idea how to ask leading questions and make insinuations that will bring this chunky Bolshevik out into the pitiless light of incriminating self-revelation. Back home on the sun-raped Salt Flats, subtlety was considered an effete, rarefied art, like harpsichord playing or versifying. Sam and his cousins never needed to be subtle when swatting brine flies off their elongated shins. So today he must fake it.

"You know something?" she bellows around a mouthful of macaroni, while staring straight at two Swiss geneticists who are having a dispute over the last saucer of brownish banana pudding. "When I was next door in China during the seven good years, the workers would usher their thinner comrades to the front of the lunch line, saying, 'Here, Comrade So-and-So, this month there is a shortage of oil for our fried noodles, and you have the most ribs of anybody among us. You go first.'"

"I'll have to take your word for that. I wasn't around, as you can probably tell."

"Oh, that's right. The Maoists also had a shortage of Americans in those days."

"What I meant," says Sam, offended, "was that I was in diapers. Rolling around in the dew on my mother's Kentucky bluegrass. Pulling adorable faces for the Brownie."

"Kentucky? But I was told you would be from the Rocky Mountains."

"Never mind. As a mere non-taxpaying American expatriate, I have no access to the agencies that could tell me what republic you're from. So we're even." First explicit lie of the day.

"Anyway, it does not matter. Look at us—" She grabs Sam's arm and twists it, so the soft, sunless underside is visible. Then she holds out her own equally flounder-pale forelimb for comparison. "See? Identical shades. We are the same. Onaji-da, as the natives so primitively put it. Even our leaders are clones. Ignorant clones both of them, handsome performers with red ball noses, like in the circus. Just clones."

129

"Clowns or clones?"

"Exactly."

Again, Sam is temporarily at a loss for words. For the lack of anything better to do, he swigs down his wine, pours more and inhales that, even though the taste is turning his tongue and teeth inside-out.

Valentina refills both of their jars, and is about to offer a toast to clones and/or clowns, when something, or someone, looming up behind Sam catches her short.

"Oh, God," she murmurs. She grabs up a few of Sam's cheese-gloppy papers and tries to hide her face. "Extreme unpleasantness approaching," she whispers to her table-mate. "Hide me, Samsha."

Sam turns and sees Jerry Lewis, again. No question, it is him. And not the current grave, wise Jerry Lewis, but the 1950's one: the crewcut, the cross-eyes, the overbite, the muscular-dystrophied knock-knees, and the smelly-socked feet that trip over any object in their path. Lugging a huge pyrex beaker brimming with something viscous as the wine, it's Jerry Lewis, right down to the idiot yell—

"Ooo-wow! Look, Dr. Val! We got it down! Ooo-wow-wow! It's ninety-nine and forty-seven one-hundredths percent pure!"

Of course, the nutty guy slips on a discarded surgical glove about ten feet away and falls flat on his face, smashing the beaker and splashing gray syrup all over the arms, faces and hair of a dozen lab-coated diners.

"Oops, sorry," he simpers, gathering himself up sheepishly. "Uh, maybe you fellas better drop by de-contam later on and take a shower or so. That's concentrated—"

"Silence!" screams Valentina. Unbelievably quick on her overburdened feet, she leaps up and pitches her research assistant out the door like a snowball. She weaves a wide circle around her puzzled, gagging colleagues, and returns to the interview, muttering unhappily under her breath in Muscovite gutter lingo, "God-damned zipperheads. Who is needing them?"

This does not bode well. Christ knows what these polar totalitarians are capable of. Sam got a miserable C-minus in high school biology. With only a little prodding he can be persuaded to imagine Hiroshimites diced to a gray froth and smeared between the jagged panes of this Muscovite's microscope slide.

Settling back down to her lunch, Valentina resumes her commentary, as if nothing untoward has taken place. "Yes, now is indeed a time for clones. You and I, Samsha, we can be big blue-eyed clones, too. We must mount a performance. We have a responsibility to let the readers of your hometown weekly gazette know that the cold war is really over, so they can get back to their births/defecations/deaths in a peaceful frame of mind. And we have an equally weighty responsibility to notify our imperious Nipponjin hosts that they are now redundant. A Pacific buffer between our two great Caucasoid civilizations is no longer necessary. These island dwarves are on their inevitable way down. Their pitiful spit-bubble has burst. Soon you and I will be riding rickshaws to work, Samsha, and paying the fare with half-smoked cigarette stubs. The natives will dive and scramble to suck the simple carbohydrates from our discarded chewing gum wrappers.

"So, please, come." She pauses, belches, hammers back her fourth jar with grace worthy of a Bolshoi ballerina, and continues. "This is not Ukrainian spiritus in our glasses. Far from it. But, no matter. Friendship is the only intoxicant we need. Together, let us now sing the Internationale."

"Um, I never really learned that one."

"Never really learned that one?" She heaves the saddest sigh of all history. "What are you doing here on Honshu besides wasting my time? Ignorant American cowboy, if they were going to insist on sending you to Asia, your party cell should have kept you strapped in the plane until it reached Mongolia, where you'd be at home with the horses. And I am saying this with an affection that wells up from my depths, Samsha."

131

"I know Chinese who were internally exiled there during the Ten Years' Chaos, and they had the time of their lives."

"Internally exiled? Where? My depths?"

"Mongolia."

"Yes, yes. I know the tale already. They learned how to ride the very mares whose milk they got chubby on, correct? Well, here is our mare's milk, Samsha. Let us get chubby on it. And meanwhile we will sing something else, just as good, in duple time."

She licks her spoon clean, puts it away, and slings her Kunming bag over her shoulder. Unflinchingly, she gropes into the coagulated mass of macaroni and cheese on Sam's trencher to switch on the microcassette recorder. Then she takes both of Sam's forearms in her hands and looks deep into his eyes.

"Please tell me you're not too immature to have heard of Pyotr Seeger. And his smash hit—"

But Sam is way ahead of her. He calls the key, and they stand up. They toast each other again in sugary Choya wine, link arms, and croon across the strange-smelling cafeteria, Valentina conducting with fingers that fling strings of cheese in wide arcs over and around their heads.

May there always be sunshine,
May there always be blue skies,
May there always be mommy,
May there always be me!

Together their rib cages swell. In unison, they suck in several dozen Nipponjins' worth of moldy Boomtown air, then exhale it, with twin facial expressions of something resembling disdain.

When the inevitable climax of physical contact does come, it's in the form of a hearty back slap: her fist explodes between this full-sized gentleman's shoulderblades like a tactical nuclear device in far-western Xinjiang. Sam only manages to stay on his feet because Valentina intertwines her elbow with his, and she is strong as a water buffalo. They remain coupled, their bodies swaying with fruity alcohol.

"Yes, we are indeed two of a kind, my Samsha. Both heartlessly betrayed by our own cultures. But here we are, like your famous Lemuel Gulliver in Lilliput, more or less productively stranded among our inferiors. I understand why I can't get a job in my country: chaotic as it is at the moment, it's hard enough to procure turnips, much less tenure. But what is your problem? What could have possessed you, my full-sized friend, at the start of such a premature decline into middle age—" She pats his gut, then strokes his pate. "—to leave the golden land of football stadium-sized supermarkets, which Yeltsin so heartily recommended to my people, and to come to this stunted, withered islet, with its fleshless citizenry, whose ribs you can catalog a city block away? You cannot tell me that all Doctors of Creative Novelization in Kentucky must leave their homes to eke out a livelihood among the yellow people."

Sam begins to wince as the subject of his unemployability in the real world is broached: the one aspect of his existence that turns him livid.

Valentina, of course, doesn't notice. She presses on, and even begins to wax rhapsodic. "I thought America was supposed to be the land of gushing milk and spewing honey, the proverbial horn of plenty, embarrassing plenty, humiliating plenty, oozing from the very skin pores of the lumpenproletariat—"

As she goes on and on, it becomes apparent that she is a slightly sloppy, oral-type drunk. Off-white triangles of suds are whipped up in the lipsticky corners of her mouth. But the overall effect of her enormous buttery presence is not so much disgusting as too rich, in the culinary sense, like certain continental steak sauces.

"Samsha, be frank with me, your fellow Caucasoid. Are all your Ph.D. classmates languishing here on the wrong side of the International Date Line? What about the women? The Hispanics? The Negroes? What about the quadriplegics and the mainstreamed mongoloids? What about the oppressed practitioners of alternative lifestyles, such as members of the gay community and pedophiles? And what about you? Don't you crave the company of other creative novelizers? Don't you miss your friends, your family, your culture?"

Sam glances around at the other diners, who, perhaps, are staring and snickering at him. "My culture?" he says. "There are whole platoons of Mormon missionaries in this town. They congregate at our place on Saturdays to watch *Little House on the Prairie* reruns on the bilingual TV. They force us to look at pictures of their big soft moms back in Provo. My culture? I get more than enough of my culture once a week. I fucking gag on it."

"But everyone knows that you Americans do not expatriate well. You become precious and catty and insufferable. I have this on good authority. It is written by your own Mr. Hem—"

The raw spot has been rubbed too hard. It wasn't in search of himself that he climbed the mountain and consulted this boozy sibyl.

"Fuck him!" screams Sam. "All the way up his tight asshole! Who's interviewing who, anyway? Jism Crust hung on the crotch!"

Of course, he is immediately chagrined at his own appalling, and slightly weird, outburst; so he starts to grovel out an apology. But, when he looks up from his sheepish shrug, he sees that Valentina's whole head, indeed, her whole upper body—not only the face, but the neck, the foot-long cleavage, the flour-sack arms, even the vast fingernails—are flushed a phosphorescent red. She is delighted by his toilet mouth.

"Now, my Samsha," she hisses huskily, pupils steaming, "yes, now you are beginning to behave like the full-sized gentleman you truly are! Come, let us visit my personal space. I will show you secret things—ah, look! As if on cue, one of my, so to speak, *patients* is arriving."

An aging day laborer is just peeking into the cafeteria, his cretinous elder sister drooling and vocalizing at his trembling elbow. Her hoots echo over the snakish sounds of Ray Conniff's golden-oldy, "Red Roses for a Blue Lady," which slithers from the Muzak.

"Let me dispose of that miserable creature, and then—ah! —we have so many things to discuss, Samsha!"

Sam's eyes are not focusing properly—grains of fructose seem to be abrading the insides of his lids—but he could swear that he sees squares of white gauze draped and patched across the woman's infant-sized face and neck. They signify, to his inflamed imagination at any rate, unrestrained tissue sampling.

He thinks he hears Valentina belch again behind his back and sigh, "Back to work. Come, Samsha, you can assist." He feels her hand on his shoulder.

A Jataka Tale Retold

Two crows are perched over the city gate, through which a learned Brahman is about to pass. The first crow says, "I'm going to shit on this guy's head."

And the second crow gasps, in horror, "But that's a learned Brahman! He's got all the sacred books memorized. He's got more power than the sun, right at his fingertips. The might of Shiva, Destroyer of Worlds, is a gnat-fart compared to what this prick can do. With a single thought he can cause our whole black-feathered tribe to disappear forever!"

To which the first crow replies, "But I must."

Argument over. Barely giving his friend time to fly away and hide in a cave, the prankster takes aim and pinches off a big one.

While it's still in mid-air, we cut to a different scene across town (a cinematic effect in a tale at least three thousand years old).

A sluggish slave girl has been charged with guarding the municipal pile of cereal as it dries in the sun. She wants to doze off, but whenever she closes her eyes, a little goat sneaks up and steals mouthfuls. So she arms herself with a torch. The next time the goat shows its face, she whacks it and sets its shaggy coat on fire.

It scampers to the royal elephant stable and rolls around in the manger to douse the flames, which spread to the walls and burn the place down, nearly killing a hundred thoroughbred elephants.

The king runs into the streets, distraught, weeping, desperate for expert advice. He sees a learned Brahman, who seems to be scraping something off his head.

"Oh, learned Brahman," cries the king, "with infinite wisdom, with the scriptures committed to memory! What magical medicine can you recommend for my hundred elephants, each one of whom I love as my own child? I have manpower at my disposal. If need be, I will levy every able-bodied subject in my kingdom to

136

scour the countryside for whatever ingredients you deem necessary. We must prepare a poultice, recondite and potent, that will soothe the vast, broiled hides of my beloved elephants. What do you prescribe?"

"Crow fat," mutters the Brahman. "Barrels and barrels of fresh crow fat."

tombradley.org

NITROSPECTIVE by Andrew Hook (Spring 2012)

Japanese school children grow giant frogs, a superhero grapples with her secret identity, onions foretell global disasters and an undercover agent is ambivalent as to which side he works for and why. Relationships form and crumble with the slightest of nudges. World catastrophe is imminent; alien invasion blasé. These twenty slipstream stories from acclaimed author Andrew Hook examine identity and our fragile existence, skid skewed realities and scratch the surface of our world, revealing another--not altogether dissimilar—layer beneath.

Nitrospective is Andrew Hook's fourth collection of short fiction and will be published during Spring 2012.
The contents are as follows:

The Onion Code
Follow Me
The Strangeness In Me
Bigger Than The Beetles
Jump
The Glass Football
Red or White
Shipping Tomorrow Backwards
Chasing Waterfalls
Lauren Is Unreal
Up
Outer Spaces
Love Is The Drug
The Cruekus Effect
Deadtime
PhotoTherapy©
Ennui
Nitrospective
Pansy Blade Cassandra Moko
Caravan of Souls
Snap Shot

RRP: £12.99 ($22.95) doghornpublishing.com/nitrospective.html